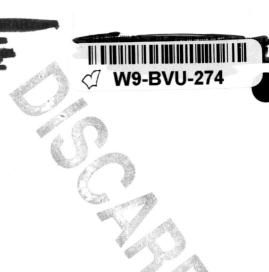
TWEED FICTION A

AGENT Q,
OR THE SMELL OF DANGER!

YOU MAY NOT HAVE GASPED AND FAINTED WHILE READING THESE OTHER THRILLING TALES OF PALS IN PERIL

Whales on Stilts!

The Clue of the Linoleum Lederhosen

Jasper Dash and the Flame-Pits of Delaware

A Pals in Peril Tale

AGENT Q

OR

THE SMELL OF DANGER!

M. T. ANDERSON

Illustrations by **KURT CYRUS**

BEACH LANE BOOKS

NEW YORK   LONDON

TORONTO   SYDNEY

BEACH LANE BOOKS
An imprint of Simon & Schuster Children's Publishing Division
1230 Avenue of the Americas, New York, New York 10020

BEACH LANE BOOKS is a trademark of Simon & Schuster, Inc.
For information about special discounts for bulk purchases, please contact
Simon & Schuster Special Sales at 1-866-506-1949
or business@simonandschuster.com.
The Simon & Schuster Speakers Bureau can bring authors to your live event.
For more information or to book an event, contact the Simon & Schuster Speakers
Bureau at 1-866-248-3049 or visit our website at www.simonspeakers.com.
The text for this book is set in Stempel Garamond.
Manufactured in the United States of America
0910 FFG
First Edition
2 4 6 8 10 9 7 5 3 1
Library of Congress Cataloging-in-Publication Data
Anderson, M. T.
Agent Q, or the smell of danger! / M. T. Anderson ; illustrations by Kurt Cyrus.—
1st ed.
p. cm.—(A pals in peril tale)
Summary: As Lily, Katie, and Jasper try to return home after their adventures
in Delaware, they face a protoplasmic monster, sleeping gas, a runaway rice cart,
sentient lobsters, and spies of the Awful and Adorable Autarch of Dagsboro.
ISBN 978-1-4169-8640-9 (hardcover : alk. paper)
[1. Adventure and adventurers—Fiction. 2. Spies—Fiction. 3. Humorous stories.
4. Mystery and detective stories.] I. Cyrus, Kurt, ill. II. Title.
PZ7.A54395Age 2010
[Fic]—dc22
2009051199
ISBN 978-1-4391-5609-4 (eBook)

With deepest affection,
this book is lovingly dedicated to

[NAME OMITTED FOR SECURITY PURPOSES]

VBNGOOM GONE

They came from the heights of the mountain, a long procession winding their way between the cracks and steeples of stone. The peak was hidden in fog. Through the ravines and over the hunched backs of granite the men padded, barefoot, all in a line, one after another, silent in the morning. They walked through the high, barren places where the ancient wind had licked the limestone into pillars and pits, caves and crevasses. There were two hundred boys and men, all dressed in flowing robes of green; and each one carried a small piece of a dismantled white van.

They marched through hollows carved by howling storms and mazes formed by

no human hand. The largest men carried the van's white doors, their heads sticking through the open windows, or they hefted a roof-panel between them. Others carried the exhaust pipe, the dashboard, the brake pads. The littlest boys—six or seven years old— carried single bolts cupped in their hands. The procession was led by two silent youths, frowning, walking side by side, both cradling the headlights in their arms. The line of them wandered through the bitter karst.

They were the monks of Vbngoom, called the Platter of Heaven, the most powerful monastery in the whole State of Delaware. They filed along dinosaur curves and great stone mounds.

Only three of the people in this solemn parade of broke-down van did not wear green robes and did not have their heads shaved.

Lily Gefelty, a slightly stocky girl whose bangs flapped down in her face or blew backward in a burst, depending on the wavering

2

breeze, carried the crankshaft timing gear. Her eyes—when they appeared through her hair—were bright, and she greeted each new vista with mute delight. She loved the mountain above them and the green forests down below. She loved that she was here with friends, and that they were on their way home after a satisfying adventure. She was very ready for home.

Behind her was Jasper Dash, Boy Technonaut. He wore a pith helmet and kept squinting into the haze, trying to make out the Delaware Canal or the smokestacks of far Wilmington. Unlike Lily, he was used to mountaintops, monks, and danger, having appeared in his own series of adventure books in which he pedaled blimps through the air, socked ruffians, and rode buffaloes bareback. Still, he also wanted to get home to his mother and his own bedroom and laboratory.

Katie Mulligan, behind him, wore the van's fan belt around her neck. She was used to adventure too, because she starred in a series

3

called Horror Hollow, in which she unwound mummies, taught werewolves to heel, and heavily salted leech invasions. Under other circumstances, she would have been grumpy about yet another adventure—she was getting tired of being bitten, stomped, and slimed—but on this particular day, she was in an extremely good mood, because right behind her walked Drgnan Pghlik, a young monk of Vbngoom who had agreed to go to the school dance with her.

It is unusual for monks to go to school dances—usually they spend their free time chanting in Latin, speaking in riddles, drawing cherubs in old books, and slapping themselves with stinging nettles—but Drgnan was a very unusual monk. For one thing, he was being trained as one of his monastery's Protectors and taught martial arts so that he could rove around the country, doing good and making sure that no pirate or plunderer threatened his sacred order and their secrets.

The monks climbed down the mountain.

They were leaving their home. Or, to be more precise, their home was leaving them.

They all gathered to rest on a little plateau with pillars of limestone like a fallen palace of wax. Lily sat down and took out her water bottle. She unscrewed the lid and took a deep swig. She watched the monks carefully. She could tell something was going to happen, but she didn't know what.

She knew that it was time for a few of the monks to leave their home so that they could go out into the world—across the forbidden border of Delaware—to collect those sculptures and gold-bound manuscripts that had recently been stolen by gangsters.* The monks would give Lily, Katie, and Jasper a ride home to Pelt, their town.

Hence the procession and the auto parts. The monks had dismantled the gangsters'

---

* As lovingly described in the previous volume, *Jasper Dash and the Flame-Pits of Delaware*.

5

white van. There was no road on this side of the mountain. They were carrying the van down the mountain to reassemble it near a road. Then Katie, Jasper, Lily, and Drgnan would drive with a few of the senior monks toward the border of Delaware. They would make their way to Pelt and reclaim the artifacts illegally sold to the Pelt Museum.

But Lily didn't understand what the rest of the holy men were doing there, or why they seemed so sad.

One of the most revered of the monks, a forty-year-old man with a clever face and an uneven grin, came over to her and her friends. His name was Grzo, and he was in charge of the Scriptorium, the room where manuscripts were copied by the monks. Usually, he spent all his days there, in a hall silent but for the squeak of quill pens and the laser-y mouth-sounds of young monks drawing angelic wars.

Brother Grzo pointed up the slope, to where the monastery could still be seen through

6

the thinning haze. He said to Drgnan, "Look up the mountain. There you see Vbngoom upon the top of Mount Tlmp for the last time."

Drgnan nodded. Lily, Jasper, and Katie looked confused and surprised. Brother Grzo explained, "Do not fear, children. You may someday see our home again, but not in this place. For two hundred years, Vbngoom has sat among the Four Peaks. It has moved among the mountains in the fog, shuffled like a pea among four nutshells to fool those who would seize upon our treasures and our sacred flames. But now that the gangsters of the World-Wide Lootery are in the hands of the government authorities, there is too much danger that we shall be found. Too many people know where our monastery is hidden. Too many roads lead to our mountaintop. Too many Delaware spies have asked too many questions. No longer can the monastery of Vbngoom hide in the clouds atop the Four Peaks. No longer is a jungle filled with kangaroo-riding cannibals and lisping serpent-men enough protection. Vbngoom must move farther away. Go and sit while we pray."

Katie, Lily, and Jasper crawled up into a small nook worn into the stone. Katie passed out sandwiches. They ate. They looked up at the towers and walls of the place they had grown to love. They watched the monks form a great circle. Some stood on rough pedestals. Out of backpacks they drew pipes and rings that they fitted together to make horns and trumpets. A few trumpeters stood aloof on pillars, awaiting a signal.

An age was coming to an end.

The abbot of the monastery, an ancient man who walked on wooden crutches, began whispering a prayer. The others joined in, each in his own time. The plateau murmured, muttered. For a long time, this went on. An hour passed. The sun moved in the sky. The shadows on the monastery walls fell crooked, then straight. The pine trees around its base wriggled in the midday sun.

And all at once, the whispering stopped—the horns came up—a great, triumphant chord echoed through the mountains, blasting away at the mirage of what was.

In the silence that followed, Lily's ears rang. No monk spoke. The abbot shuffled out to the middle of the ring of monks. He looked up at his home. He raised his palm and lay it beneath his lips. And he blew.

That tiny breath traveled up the mountainside—hit the pine trees like a gale—and the monastery began to unravel as if it was made of dry sand. Away flew a turret—and now walls were sifting off in clouds, blowing through the sky, brilliant, glittering—all of it—the trees on the peak, the volcanic crater, the cloisters, the bridges, the chapels, the banners—all of it swarmed through the air, locustlike, and tumbled off to the north.

Vbngoom migrated through the sky.

Lily cried at it shimmering in the noonday light.

Then there was no more monastery there—in fact, no more peak. Suddenly the monks were only a quarter mile from the top.

The kids were sad that Vbngoom could no longer stay atop Mount Tlmp, but glad it would be safe elsewhere.

Drgnan came to their side, wiping his eyes. The musicians were unscrewing their trumpets and dismantling their pipes and stowing them in backpacks. The rest said quick prayers and picked up their automotive parts.

Then the procession set off again, holding high their tappets, their clutch, their shocks.

Vbngoom was gone.

A Spy in the Salad

As every schoolchild knows, Delaware, the Blue Hen State, located between Pennsylvania, Maryland, and New Jersey, is ruled by a tyrant known only as His Terrifying Majesty, the Awful and Adorable Autarch of Dagsboro. He is crazy and cruel. He has a large, starched mustache like a Prussian general of the nineteenth century. He sits in his palace just outside of Dover and frets about how he can ensure that he will rule the state for all time. His spies, sent out by the feared Ministry of Silence, peer into every living room and squat under tables at every bar, listening for talk of rebellion.*

And in that city of Dover, amid the narrow alleys and the temples and the towers, one of those spies, Bntno, came home after a long day at work. His flip-flops dragged on the flagstones.

Bntno worked as an informer. This meant that he took out-of-state tourists on trips and spied on them for the Awful and Adorable Autarch of Dagsboro. He reported to the Ministry of Silence. It was not always an easy job. He had to conceal from the tourists that anything was rotten in the State of Delaware. That morning a couple from Texas had noticed that all the newspapers had articles cut out of them. In the

---

*Am I getting this right? I would hate it if my portraits of people from Delaware were in any way mistaken or misleading. If you are actually from Delaware, and you feel that there are inaccuracies in my portrayal of your state, I hope that you will write a note explaining the error, hop on your ostrich, ride through the jungle to the nearest mail rocket, have the Censor from the Ministry of Silence read your letter and cross out the illegal parts, clap it into the belly of the missile, and send it winging on its way into the civilized world.

afternoon, a group of Idahoan senior citizens had asked why all the kids at one school were shackled together in a line. They did not believe that the children were happy, even though all the children wore paper smiley faces.

It had been a long day. Bntno trod wearily up the steps to his apartment. The building was made of concrete and stained with soot. Flies were caught in the windows, and they rattled.

The informer let himself into his apartment and shut the door behind him. He locked three locks and a chain. For a minute he just stood, exhausted, in his dark living room. He wished he never had to talk to another out-of-state tourist again. Just a few days before, he had taken some very troublesome children, yes, very troublesome, all the way through the jungle to the Four Peaks. They had not even thanked him, not even when he pointed a gun at them. Very rude. Yes, troublesome children. They had escaped him. It made him tired.

He headed for the kitchen to get a drink.

He had made it most of the way across the living room carpet when he heard a noise. Not much—just someone shifting position. A slight rattle. Immediately, he looked around warily.

He threw himself into the kitchen.

No one. Sink. Drain. Counters. Cabinets. Stove.

He bobbed back out into the living room. No one.

But in the pile of the rug he saw footprints. Someone had been walking through his apartment.

He frowned. He backed into the kitchen, against the refrigerator door. He decided to pretend nothing was wrong.

Slowly, carefully, he opened the refrigerator, peering around, and reached for a cool bottle of Tyrant Splash.

He jumped back in surprise. Secret Agent Mrglik was curled up in the fridge, writing notes.

Agent Mrglik looked up from his work. "Ah, Bntno. I'm glad you could come."

"Ah—well—the gentleman spy is . . . in my kitchen."

"And my feet are in your crisper. Still, there's work to be done." Mrglik swung his legs out and stood. "Bntno, we at the Ministry of Silence are not very pleased with you."*

This struck terror into Bntno's heart. Delaware's Ministry of Silence was brutal and inefficient.

Mrglik half turned and began whisking a leftover Caesar salad off his rump. "Last week,"

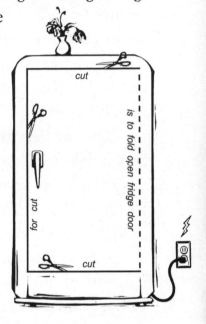

cut

is to fold open fridge door

for cut

cut

---

*I have translated all of the following dialogue from the original Doverian (the ancient tongue of Delaware). I had the help of a battered Doverian/English dictionary and a nice waiter at our local Delawarian restaurant, the Blue Hen Pantry. Prdo, the waiter, tells me my Doverian is not very good. The other day when I ordered a succulent Delawarian delicacy—flying squirrel on Triscuits—he slapped me with his order pad. I protested. He pointed out that I had dropped two syllables and switched a third, so I had not said, "Friend, please bring me the squirrel crackers," but, "Hit me hard with paper, mister, special quick!"

he stated, "you led three out-of-state children north to try to find the monastery of Vbngoom, the Platter of Heaven." Caesar dressing and anchovies splattered on the floor. Mrglik removed a few wilted pieces of lettuce from his pants and dropped them in the sink. "You were to report on the location of Vbngoom so that His Terrifying Majesty could sweep in with his army."

"Yes, sir. Very troublesome children. They gave me the slip."

"Well do we know!" cried a voice. "Well do we know of your failure!"

Bntno looked around wildly. It wasn't Mrglik.

"Officer Blozcz," explained Mrglik, opening one of the cabinet doors to reveal his colleague hunkered among the pots and pans.

"Good day, Officer Blozcz," said Bntno, clutching his hands together. "I hope you are well."

"I am not well," said Blozcz, "when enemies of our glorious state are free."

"I apologize deeply to the gentlemen that I let the children escape."

"The children do not matter," said Mrglik. "We do not seek the children, but the monks and their monastery."

Officer Blozcz said, "The monastery contains not only great riches, but also the mystical Flame-Pits where the soldiers of our jolly, friendly army could be trained to become psychic warriors. For the uplift of the thankful, happy people of this State."

"Psychic warrior-spies with the power," said Mrglik, making his hand float above his other hand, "of levitation and reading the minds and sending thoughts without words."

"What do you wish me to do, gentlemen?"

said Bntno, backing up against the stove fearfully.

A muffled voice said, "This morning we sent a plane . . . Mrglik?"

Mrglik explained, "The excellent Commissar Dlvlo is in the lazy susan." He swung the lazy susan open. Commissar Dlvlo slid into sight.

"Thank you, Agent," said Commissar Dlvlo, curled up, smoothing the sides of her tweed skirt.

"My pleasure, Commissar," said Mrglik.

"Yes," said Bntno, getting impatient. "Maybe it is time to show me everyone who hides in my kitchen?"

Agent Mrglik looked to Commissar Dlvlo for approval. She nodded, and Mrglik went along the counter, opening all the cupboards. There were agents and officers crouched in each one.

Commissar Dlvlo continued, "This morning we flew a plane over the Four Peaks, where the monastery of Vbngoom supposedly is hidden. You have told us the monastery is there.

The gangsters of the World-Wide Lootery, who are in our prison, tell us that the monastery is in those mountains. But we could not find it—not head nor hair. It is nowhere to be found. So we must be clever, with our smart hats." She tapped her head. "We believe that the out-of-state children you have met will seek to cross the border to return to their homes. And we believe that monks of Vbngoom will try to help them."

"We believe that two or three monks," explained a man in the canned goods, "plan to leave the state to deliver the children home and reclaim the monastery's treasures."

"But they cannot be allowed to slip away," said a man in the snack foods. "Because they know the location of Vbngoom."

"And the location," said Blozcz in pots and pans, "of all of the treasures that were plundered by the gangsters of the World-Wide Lootery."

"So they must be apprehended," said snack

foods. "They must be apprehended and questioned," he proclaimed, almost wailing, rattling the Cheetos in agony like a vengeful ghost.

"Now," said Commissar Dlvlo, glowering and businesslike. "We suspect they will head north through the Montchanin Valley and attempt to cross the border at Guyencourt. This is the easiest route. I have called the border police at Guyencourt. I have spoken to them at length. I have given them instructions and descriptions of the children. Though I am in a lazy susan, I am not lazy." She reached out, clutched the walls, and wheeled herself around. When she reappeared on the other side of the lazy susan, she had a computer printout on her knees. "We have stepped up the security in Guyencourt. It is a small town. No one can pass by there unnoticed. The monks and the children will walk right into our clutches."

"We need you, however," said a crackly voice.

"Who is that voice?" said Bntno.

"That is Control, the head of the Ministry of Silence," said Agent Mrglik.

"Control is in the salt," said Dlvlo.

Mrglik picked up the saltshaker and adjusted it. "Control? Can you hear us? Greetings to Control."

The lid came off. Salt went all over the floor.

"Pepper," said Commissar Dlvlo. "He is in the pepper. I am of a hope I do not misremember and he is in the Parmesan."

Mrglik adjusted the reception on the pepper shaker, at which point Control said, "Informant Bntno, you will go north in a small plane with Agent Mrglik. You will drive up and down the Montchanin Valley, and there you shall assist the police and the border guards in finding these children and their monks. You know their faces. We wish you to find them for us."

"Do not fail us, Informant Bntno," said Commissar Dlvlo, her arms, braced against the wall of the lazy susan, raised on either side of her as if she were casting some evil spell. "Do not fail us. We will be waiting here. We will be watching." With a frightening look, she swung herself around and disappeared.

Bntno nodded. He said, "Please do not eat all my Teddy Grahams."

Through the door, she explained, "We will not be waiting in your lazy susan. We wait in our headquarters. Our HQ. Understood?"

Bntno nodded. He was sure he could capture those children.

In an hour, he and Mrglik were taking off and flying over the jungle where he had last seen Katie, Jasper, and Lily. In two hours, he was passing over the Four Peaks, over Mount Tlmp, where no monastery now stood. He scanned the heights but saw nothing. It didn't matter, he thought to himself; in any case, they'd find out where the monastery was soon enough.

In three hours, he was high above the Montchanin Valley and, like the children, was headed for the border of Delaware.

THE PLAN WITH THE VAN

Winding their way down the north face of Tlmp, the monks passed through an oak savannah on a slant. The grasses were golden, the few trees hazy with light. Great boulders, larger than houses, reared up out of the meadow. The late afternoon sun caught on the crests of the duck-billed dinosaurs that browsed on the leaves.

Lily was sorry they were leaving all this behind.

She knew all the monks were sorry to leave Tlmp. They would walk on to their new home, where Vbngoom now rested, empty, somewhere in the impassable Newark Range to the northwest.

The monks would wend their way up into new mountains. They would pass through new forests. They would find their ancient home crouched upon a new peak, its blue flames burning at its heart to welcome them.

That is, this is what they would find if the Awful and Adorable Autarch of Dagsboro didn't find them first. They knew he sought them.

So, silent, brooding, the procession continued down the mountainside.

When the evening fell, Lily sat listening to the lonely honking of the duck-billed dinosaurs from hilltop to hilltop. The gentle, lumbering beasts swished through the steep red pampas as the monks wove dinners out of grass.

As Lily and Katie wandered around the camp, watching the preparations for the evening, Katie asked, "So what do you think of Drgnan? Isn't he great?"

Lily nodded. She thought Drgnan was very great. "He's really nice," she said.

"I can't believe he agreed to go to the dance with me." Katie swung one of her arms around to get a crick out of her shoulder. "What do you think is the best thing about him? Of all the things?"

Lily shrugged. She thought hard about Drgnan. "There's a lot of great things about him," she said. "I mean, he's really kind, and he listens to you when you talk, and—"

"He's funny, too, isn't he?"

"Yeah, he's funny."

"And he's really cute."

"Yeah. He is," said Lily. She kept thinking about how good-looking he was.

Katie said, "He really knows how to wear a robe. He never looks stupid or awkward in it. Like, if I had to wear a robe the whole time? I'd always be tripping over it. And I'd come out of the bathroom with the back of it tucked into my underpants."

Lily agreed, "He's really graceful." She frowned. "And he's gentle."

"And he has those eyes," said Katie. "It looks like he sees through you. Into your *soul*, you know? Your whole *soul*?" She put her hands together and made a kind of praying, pushing, diving motion with her hands, as if he were actually plunging into her soul from a high board and crashing into the blue, clear waters of her spirit.

Lily said, "It's really great that he thinks a lot about spiritual things." She shrugged with one shoulder.

"He's amazing," said Katie. "I could talk about him for another five hours."

"We should go find him and Jasper," said Lily. "We need to set up our tents."

Later that night, as she lay in her sleeping bag, listening to the lonely cries of the dinosaurs on the savannah, Lily thought about Katie and Drgnan.

Lily had never gone out with anyone. It was exciting to watch other people get crushes on each other, but it seemed like something that would never happen to her. Since fourth grade, she had occasionally had a little crush on some kid at school—Myron, for example, in her sixth-grade homeroom, whose thumbs were double-jointed and who could draw really amazing leopards; or, this year, Stuart, her study buddy from earth science class—but those were just stupid little pangs, and they didn't matter much to her. She was too shy to really talk much to those boys. She hid behind her hair. She knew she wasn't pretty, like Katie. Somehow, it seemed like only the pretty people really *deserved* to have their crushes work out.

She hadn't thought about it much before.

And now it made her uncomfortable that she thought Drgnan was so great. So, so great. So amazingly, stupendously great. So great that she wished she could—

But she had to be happy for Drgnan and Katie. They were two of her favorite people, and they really liked each other. Finally, here was a boy who Lily thought deserved someone as wonderful as Katie.

So why didn't she feel happier about it?

Lily turned over and buried her face in the foam pillow. She made a silent vow that she would be absolutely thrilled for her two friends. No sulking. No wistfulness.

After all, it was super for everyone.

Outside, in the night, the duck-billed herbivores curled together beneath the oaks and succumbed to quacky, snoring slumber. Night was thick above the grasslands and the boulders, the foothills of the mountains. The stars turned in the heavens.

The monks' lookouts sat, staring into the night and eating apples.

Everyone slept.

The next morning they reached the great eucalyptus forests lower on the slopes, where they spied herds of centaurs watching their progress through the huge, spotted trees. The forest floor was woven with slivers of bark that smelled richly of earth and mint. In front of Lily, Katie and Drgnan were whispering and giggling, and Lily watched them with a kind of melancholy contentment. She told herself that she was happy for them. Jasper, of course, was in his element on a hike like this and kept putting his fists on his hips and taking measurements of the sun and the barometric pressure. He couldn't wait to tell Lily his findings ("We're headed north by northeast"), and she listened with pleasure.

At one point, she asked him, "Jasper . . . do you and Drgnan talk?"

She was wondering what Drgnan thought about Katie. She hoped Drgnan liked Katie back. For Katie's sake. She really hoped it.

Jasper looked at her oddly. "Of course we talk."

Lily said nervously, "What about? Like, personal things?"

"Why, we talk about everything."

"Do you ever talk about . . ." Lily couldn't make herself go on. She was too embarrassed. She just said, "Like what?"

"Well, we have heart-to-hearts . . . about . . . you know . . . what you and Katie probably talk about: what tattoos we'll get when we're older. Which of us can slap higher on a wall. What the rules would be for a ball game with bikes that spit fire."

"Tattoos?" Lily said. She blinked in surprise, scraping away at her long bangs. "So what tattoos will you get?"

"I'd like to have a bolt of energy. Or maybe an atom on my chest. Drgnan wants an infinity sign with googly eyes."

Lily thought about that for a minute. "You know," she said, "he might be sorry about that one day."

"That's what I told him," Jasper agreed. "So I suggested he just get the infinity sign, and then he can use stick-on, adhesive googly eyes."

"That's a really good idea," Lily admitted, finding that the conversation had ended up in kind of a different place than she had hoped.

Jasper hopped along until he was beside Drgnan. "Drgnan, my good fellow, Drgnan—I would give a silver solenoid to know where we're going."

Drgnan explained to them, "Brother Grzo has not told me much. We are going down the mountain to reassemble the van. Brother Grzo himself shall drive it. Then we will head for the border."

"Which border?" asked Jasper.

Drgnan explained, "There are three routes out of Delaware to the north."* He counted them on his fingers. "There is a ferry from the great city of Wilmington that takes people to New Jersey. But the government watches carefully to see who comes and who leaves by this boat. The Ministry of Silence would stop us. This would be bad—very bad—because the Awful and Adorable Autarch of Dagsboro hunts always for monks from Vbngoom, to find out our secrets. So there are two other routes. One is the Newport Gap Pike, which leads through the Newark Mountains and across the Newark Steppe. It provides dangerous passage to hearty merchants from Kaolin who wish to take their wares to Elsmere and Minquadale. But it is a cold and a high road, and no van could drive across it."

"Why do we need the van?" asked Katie.

"So we can pick up all the treasures scattered

---

*You can see them on the map at the beginning of the book.

across the whole East Coast and return with them," explained Drgnan. "We need a van. So we shall go straight north, up the Montchanin Road, and shall cross the border at the little village of Guyencourt, where the guards are sleepy and the dogs are fat."

He did not realize that in the previous chapter, the Autarch's spies had guessed the monks would take exactly this route. He did not know he was describing an itinerary of catastrophe. He had not read the previous chapter at all.

"Hey," said Katie, who was always skeptical of something. "Why is it that most *people's* names in this state don't have hardly any vowels in them, but a lot of the names of places do?"

Drgnan nodded sadly. "Since the Adorable Autarch seized power here, the other states have placed a vowel embargo on Delaware. For many years, no vowels—*a*, *e*, *i*, *o*, *u*, or sometimes even *y*—have come into this state. So no new names have those letters in them. The place names are old, but the people are young, and we have no vowels to spare."

"Okay. This is just stupid, because you're using all kinds of vowels when you talk."

"N 'm nt," said Drgnan, small-mouthed.

"What?"

"'m nt sng vwls."

Katie scrunched up her mouth and looked at him hard.

Jasper started laughing.

Katie thought about this for a minute. "Okay!" she said triumphantly. "Okay, what about this? If all the place-names have vowels because they're old, then why does Vbngoom, the oldest place around, have missing vowels?"

"It had vowels. Years ago."

"Oh, really."

"Yes, indeed. We gave them to the poor."

Katie scowled. "You . . . !" she declared indignantly.

Drgnan looked off innocently into the blue sky.

Katie whipped the back of his head with a strip of eucalyptus.

By the next day, the wood had grown thicker, and so had the air. It smelled of some kind of laurel, which was (Lily sniffed) kind of like the smell of spicy food burnt. She loved the green. They were marching through the foothills of the mountains.

Lily and some of the monks were getting apprehensive. They were approaching civilization. And soon they would come back within the view of the Autarch's spies.

Now, finally, there were signs of mankind. Occasionally they passed the huts of hermits. Then, a few hours later, they came to small farms where kids stood near split-rail fences and watched the silent monks in wonder. Then, an hour or two after that, they came to their first village.

An old man in a straw hat joined them as if by some agreement. He led them to his barn. The procession walked into the barn on one side and right out the other door. But when they came out, they no longer had their pieces of the van.

Without so much as a pause, they started to walk back into the forest.

But they left several behind: among them, Drgnan Pghlik, Brother Grzo, Lily, Katie, and Jasper.

From the barn came the sound of ratcheting and tinkering.

A hundred and ninety-six monks, small and tall, walked away to the west. They spoke to no one. They were off to the Newark Mountains to rejoin their monastery on its new peak.

"That's that," said Katie.

Lily said, "I'm sorry to see them go."

"We're on our way home, though!" Katie urged her, grinning.

Lily nodded. "I'm glad," she said. "I'm kind of tired."

"Sure," said Katie. "But we're almost out of here. We have the van. What could go wrong now?"

"What, indeed, children?" said Brother Grzo, coming up behind them and putting his hands on their shoulders, smiling his crooked smile. "Once we have passed through the Pulaski Forest and the Montchanin Valley, as long as we are not attacked by bandits or trolls, and once we— . . . ah, or manticoras—bandits, trolls, or manticoras—or lions—bandits, trolls, manticoras, lions, wolves, bears, basilisks, flying squirrels, or nightmare dolls—"

"Okay," said Katie.

". . . and once we have eluded the government agents who will seek to arrest us and torture us to get us to tell them where the monastery has gone, and once we have brought you across the border secretly without being recognized as monks or imprisoned deep in the dungeons of Fort Delaware with only a trickle of scum to drink and whatever toads leap in our lap to eat, and—"

"All righty," said Katie.

"Well, then we shall be driving free as the plover flies, singing songs of ecstasy. Oh, joyous Brother Sun!"

Suddenly, thought Lily, the odds didn't sound so great.

On the Road

Driving with monks was fun. Lily could not remember a better road trip. The four kids sat in the back of the van, playing cards. Katie kept losing and shrieking about it happily, punching Drgnan softly in the shoulder.

Lily watched out the window as they came to the Delaware Canal. It was wide, brown, and smooth. They crossed a great stone bridge at a town called St. Georges, a collection of crazed half-timbered houses hanging over the river. Fishermen lay in hammocks slung between the stilts, their lines trailing. In a wide concrete plaza there was a market going on. People in robes and spiny hats sold citrus fruits from boxes. Bicycles loaded with geese joggled along muddy lanes.

While the kids and the monks ate lunch at a barbecue stand, Brother Grzo questioned the people at the picnic tables around them about border security at Guyencourt. "We wish to cross the border. In these days, how firm is the fist of the tyrant there?"

A merchant shrugged. "Not so bad. Unless they are searching for you. Then"—he shivered—"then I would not like to imagine. I watched a whole caravan drive into the security checkpoint and never come out the other side. I still, to this day, do not know where it went."

The monks and the kids did not stay long in St. Georges. After lunch, they got back in the van, waved out the window at a few friends in the market, then drove north into the depths of the Pulaski Forest. Soon the trees were tall and the wood was dark.

One of the best things about road-tripping with monks is that monks are used to repeating chants over and over and over, so they really don't mind songs like "Ninety-nine Bottles of

Beer on the Wall" or "The Song That Never
Ends."

If you don't know "The Song That Never
Ends," let me just remind you. It's the one that
goes:

This is the song that never ends,

It just goes on and on, my friends.

Some people started singing it, not knowing what it was,

And they'll continue singing it forever just because

This is the song that never ends,

It just goes on and on, my friends.

Some people started singing it, not knowing what it was,

And they'll continue singing it forever just because

This is the song that never ends,

It just goes on and on, my friends.

Some people started singing it, not knowing what it was,

And they'll continue singing it forever just because

This is the song that never ends,

It just goes on and on, my friends.

Some people started singing it, not knowing what it was,

And they'll continue singing it forever just because

This is the song that never ends,

It just goes on and on, my friends.

Some people started singing it, not knowing what it was,

And they'll continue singing it forever just because

This is the song that never ends,

It just goes on and on, my friends.

Some people started singing it, not knowing what it was,

And they'll continue singing it forever just because

This is the song that never ends,

It just goes on and on, my friends.

Some people started singing it, not knowing what it was,

And they'll continue singing it forever just because

This is the song that never ends,

It just goes on and on, my friends.

Some people started singing it, not knowing what it was,

And they'll continue singing it forever just because

This is the song that never ends,

It just goes on and on, my friends.

Some people started singing it, not knowing what it was,

And they'll continue singing it forever just because

This is the song that never ends,

It just goes on and on, my friends.

Some people started singing it, not knowing what it was,

And they'll continue singing it forever just because

This is the song that never ends,

It just goes on and on, my friends.

Some people started singing it, not knowing what it was,

And they'll continue singing it forever just because

This is the song that never ends,

It just goes on and on, my friends.

Some people started singing it, not knowing what it was,

And they'll continue singing it forever just because

This is the song that never ends,

It just goes on and on, my friends.

Some people started singing it, not knowing what it was,

And they'll continue singing it forever just because

This is the song that never ends,

It just goes on and on, my friends.

Some people started singing it, not knowing what it was,

And they'll continue singing it forever just because . . .

As Jasper, Katie, and Drgnan shouted it at the top of their lungs for mile after mile, passing Dragon Creek and the village of Corbit, the monks in the front didn't complain. They rocked their heads in time with the music.

Brother Grzo said, "Is not all life a song that never ends?"

And his friend replied, "And are we not each just one verse?"

The third monk, Bvletch, was not as generous. Though he was, deep down, a very kind and loving monk, he was sixteen—a teenager— so he had just taken his Vow of Sarcasm. This meant that for two years, he had to say nothing that wasn't ironic and snotty. So he sat there grumbling, "Wow. This is great. I love this. I hope it goes on all night. When do you cut your first album? Sure. Awesome. This fills me with a joy like the bee alighting on a flower to drink its sweet nectar. Hey, could you sing that verse again? A little louder?" etc.*

And so they did sing it louder, until Lily broke in and said, "Hey . . . hey, we should stop. Because I think Bvletch isn't very happy."

The other three stopped. "Yes," said Drgnan. "We do not wish to cause sorrow to Bvletch. We shall not sing 'The Song That Never Ends' anymore." There was a moment of silence where the van rattled and squeaked and everyone could hear themselves breathe before Drgnan said joyfully, "Instead we shall sing 'The Littlest Worm I Ever Saw.'" And he and Katie busted into "The Littlest Worm," which left teen Blvetch crumpled under the seat, his thumbs in his ears.

They were passing through a little village, some wattle-and-daub houses with thatched

---

*Most of the monks of Vbngoom take the Vow of Sarcasm as teenagers. When the two sarcastic years are over, then they never tell a lie or say anything mean ever again. They've gotten it out of their systems.

If you have an older brother or sister, you may have noticed that they, too, have taken a Vow of Sarcasm.

roofs gathered around a square. As they drove through the square, past an old tractor and a statue of St. George, people looked up from their work—washerwomen at their buckets, the butcher with his cleaver, a dentist performing a curbside root canal—and sullenly watched the van rattle through town.

"Wave! Everyone wave!" cried Grzo, and he waved furiously out the window. Jasper and Katie waved too, and the dentist smiled toothlessly and waved back. "Say hello!" cried Grzo, smiling his crooked smile, and the whole van shouted glad greetings, except, of course, Bvletch, who rolled his eyes and said, "Great. It's candy hour at the Sore-Head Saloon. Give me double my nougat."

He was not yet very good at sarcasm. He still had some work to do.

They came at last to the village of Red Lion on the banks of Red Lion Creek. They pulled up in front of the Red Lion Inn, which was a kind of strange, shingled tower, like a lighthouse that had forgotten to dress itself with ocean and had put on dirt skirts instead. It had lots of pokey, round windows and balconies, and a sign over the door showing a scarlet lion standing up on its hind legs and clawing the air.

Grzo turned off the engine and opened the door. "We have business here," he said. "You, precious children, stay near to the van. All monks, we must go into the inn for a time."

Everyone climbed out of the van, stretching their legs and cracking their joints. Jasper bent down and touched his toes, then swung back and forth, arms bent. All of them were hot and a little sore from the walking and riding.

"We will not be a minute," said Grzo. "If the chicks will stay in the nest, the wren shall return with the plump worm for feasting."

Katie looked at Red Lion Creek, where it flowed sweetly through the dell. "Yeah. Hold the worms. But can we sit by the river?" she asked. "I want to cool off."

"Yes, certainly," said Brother Grzo. "But be wary, dear child."

Katie, Jasper, and Lily went down to the bank of the creek. The four monks—the two adults, teen Bvletch, and young Drgnan—promised to come back as quickly as possible. They processed into the inn.

Katie kicked off her shoes and sank her heels into the cool moss. "I really want to go in for a swim," she said.

"I wouldn't, Katie," said Jasper. "Brother Grzo told us to be wary."

"He didn't say anything about not going into the river. 'Wary' doesn't mean 'dry.'"

She looked around and spotted an old man sitting nearby on a mildewed beach chair, whittling. He whistled slowly to himself in the green shade.

"Hey," said Katie. "Sir?"

He looked up, smiled, and replied in Doverian.

"I'm sorry," said Katie. "Do . . . you . . . speak . . . English?"

46

He nodded and wriggled his hand. "Little English," he said cheerfully.

"Can I go in the river?"

He looked at the river, looked at her, shrugged, nodded.

She waded in up to her knees. She called back to him, "There isn't anything I should worry about, is there?" she said. "I mean, bandits, trolls, wolves, bears, nightmare dolls . . . ?"

The old man said, "No, small miss. No fear. Lion Creek . . . Lion Creek, it going by many of this Autarch's factories, many big factories, so nothing, no, nothing alive in it here. No fish, no shark, no crocodemon. All dead. Nothing but one-cell organism." He held up a single finger. "Nothing else live."

"Is that good news?" asked Katie, looking at the water skeptically.

Lily said, "I wouldn't get any in your mouth, from the sounds of things."

Katie decided she'd better not go in any

farther. She wriggled her toes in the mud. She splashed her legs.

Jasper was up rummaging around in the van. Lily sat by the side of the creek. It was a pleasant hollow, with water rushing over the rocks and trees hanging low around the banks. It was not a bad place to sit for a while.

Katie was doing high kicks and spraying herself with water. "I wish Drgnan didn't have to go inside with them," she said. "He'd be fun to splash."

Lily asked shyly, "Are you looking forward to going to the dance with him?"

"It's going to be great. He *floats in the air* when he dances, Lily."

Lily smiled. She looked up at Katie doing pirouettes in the ripples.

And screamed.

Something huge had risen up behind her friend. Something blobby. Something with shuddering, hungry little tendrils all over it.

BLOB VIOLENCE

The blob heaved.

Katie half turned—saw the thing—yelped—
and stumbled toward shore—each step slow as a
nightmare—each step plowing through current—
each throwing up a claw of spray.

She struggled toward the bank.

Lily saw the monster flex itself and prepare
to engulf her friend. She didn't know what to
do—but she grabbed a stick from the shore and
waded in, waving it.

Jasper looked down toward the creek—he saw
them. "Great Scott!" he exclaimed. He grabbed
his rucksack and began searching desperately for
his ray gun. He tore through the useless contents
of his pack—he swore by all the major moons of

Jupiter in ascending order of their orbits—"Io, Europa, Ganymede, and Callisto!"—but could lay his hands on nothing but beef jerky and plaid underwear. He kept digging.

Lily was almost by Katie's side, holding the tree branch defiantly. "Get back!" Katie cried to Lily.

And at that moment, the blob lunged.

Lily jabbed. Katie jumped. The butt of the stick slapped into the monster's clear flesh and knocked it aside for a moment. Katie spun away, and the monster splashed into the water.

Katie and Lily looked down into the river. The monster was translucent—there was no way to see it, once it was underwater. They began to dash for the shore. Katie grabbed another branch trapped in the rocks. She yanked it free and brandished it.

On the shore, Jasper found his travel pillow.

Katie saw a motion—turned her head—and found the monster towering out of the river, its transparent flesh gleaming in the sun.

She poked it with her stick. It moved toward her, wobbling hungrily.

"Side to side!" Lily screamed.

Katie didn't understand what Lily was talking about. The monster dropped toward her. She tripped backward. It fell on top of her.

The slime was all over her. The world was wrinkled and wavery through the monster's clear skin. Katie couldn't breathe. She fell to her knees. She struggled to beat the beast, but it was all around her. She rolled, and was lying on her back, her legs in the water and her head in the blob.

And suddenly she realized what Lily meant.

The blob was trying to draw her completely into itself so it could digest her. If the stick went side to side, she would be too wide. The monster wouldn't be able to engulf her totally. The blob was folded over her like a pancake, but she was not yet fully inside of it.

She yanked the stick so it went side to side. The monster struggled to pull her into its flesh. It couldn't get around the ends of the branch. It was stretching itself thin.

Lily was up above, prying at the thing, using her stick as a lever.

Katie struggled to breathe.

On the shore, Jasper found his sandals.

The monster shuddered and tried to digest. It couldn't fit Katie. It heaped itself and scrunched. With the *shlup* of a boot pulled out of Mississippi mud, Katie's head popped out of the blob.

She was lying, her back on the sand, trying to keep her head above the couple of inches of water. She kicked. She boxed at the monster with her branch. It stretched itself in one direction and then another. She thwacked and pedaled. It warped and leaped. She was disgusted by its clingy, pulpy touch, its writhing and slapping. Lily whacked it with her stick.

The monster bunched. It slithered. It gulped.

Katie thrust out her hand—spread the blob's flesh—stretched it as thin as pizza dough!

And the blob, pulled out of shape, quivering with protoplasmic rage, dropped off her.

The water ran over Katie, and the monster let itself be pulled away with it. It dribbled downstream.

It was gone.

The two girls crawled out of the river onto the bank.

Jasper finally dodged down to their side, holding his ray gun aloft. He looked around for his enemy. "Dash it all!" he said.

"We're okay," said Lily. "Thank you anyway."

Katie screamed at the old man on the rotting chair, *I thought you said there weren't any creatures in this river!*"

"Excellent, forceful miss, I say that there are only one-cell organism, yes? And that was a one-cell organism. I think amoeba."

"An amoeba is LITTLE," said Katie, squinching her fingers together. "Little. Teeny tiny."

AMOEBA
(Amoeba proteus supergiganticus)

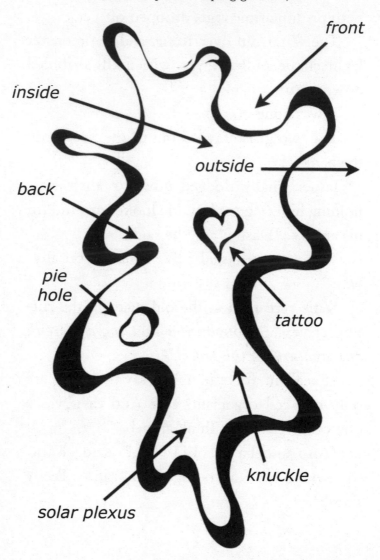

front

inside

outside

back

pie
hole

tattoo

knuckle

solar plexus

"That one, it seem big to me," said the old man, shrugging. "Not so tiny."

"I *know*," said Katie. "I was almost *drowned* by it."

"Not so tiny, I say."

Katie exhaled angrily and stomped across the pebbles and up the slope to try and find a towel.

In a minute the monks came back from the inn, carrying sandwiches and drinks for dinner. "Good, good," said Grzo. "We are done. I hope you have enjoyed . . . You swam? Not so good an idea. Many one-celled—"

"I know," growled Katie. She shot an angry glance at the old man on the old chair. The old man on the old chair waved an old hand and smiled a young smile.

The moment Drgnan discovered what had happened, he ran down to the riverbank and joined Jasper, peering up and down the current, looking for the blob to bash it.

"Come, children!" Grzo called down to

them. "We must hurry if we are to reach Guy-encourt on schedule. Just three days, and many miles to cross."

The boys, disappointed that they didn't have a chance to whomp a monster, trudged back up to the van and climbed in. Shortly the van was jouncing across the river on a bridge guarded by stone lions.

The old man on his rotten chair watched them go. Then he stood up, lay down his whit-tling, and scampered into a barber shop. Scissors were clickety-clacking. Bangs were falling. He went into the back and dialed a number on the phone.

In Doverian, he whispered, "Hello. Hello. This is Informant Pmnd. I have been advised to call if any monks of Vbngoom were seen on Route One. I have just seen four monks in the green robes of Vbngoom. They are in a white van with three children. The children are from out of state. I heard them speak. They are all headed north to Guyencourt. They plan to cross the border three days from now. Yes. Yes. Thank you. For my free gift, I would like E-352. That is the watermelon boom box. If supplies have not lasted, I would like the walking-an-invisible-dog trick leash. Number . . ." He pulled out a grimy, wrinkled old catalogue and flipped through it. He left his information and hung up.

He went out again to sit by the river and whittle.

A few weeks from now, he thought, *brother, I tell you! I'll be sitting here listening to some sweet, juicy tunes.*

THE PROBLEM WITH HAVING
A FRIEND WHO'S IN LOVE

"I spy," said Jasper, "with my little eye, something . . . that begins with *F*."

It turned out to be a fungus on a tree. Drgnan guessed it.

Drgnan said, "I spy . . . with my little eye . . . somethinnnnnnnng . . ."

Katie stared at Drgnan's eyes. They were not little. They were large and beautiful. She wished she could see out of them.

". . . that begins," said Drgnan. "With."

"It is a shame," Jasper mused, "that we are not in a wood with pteranodons. Because no one would guess pteranodons."

Lily said, "Let Drgnan pick his letter."

"*H*," said Drgnan.

They thought for a minute.

"Hill?" suggested Lily.

"Hawk?" said Jasper, who didn't see one himself, but still hoped.

"Hottie?" said Katie, also hopefully.

Then she realized what she had said, and blushed.

It turned out to be a hophornbeam. Drgnan explained it was a kind of tree. "A hophornbeam?!?" Katie protested. "No one knows what a hophornbeam is! That should just be *T* for tree!"

"Then you have the next turn, my sister."

Needless to say, her turn was *E*.

For eyes.

"Drgnan's," she said.

When she explained, Drgnan looked nervous. And Katie herself, now that she had said it out loud, suddenly looked embarrassed.

Blvetch rolled over from his nap and said, in no uncertain terms, "I spy, with my little eye, something that begins with 'stupid.'"

THE HAIR OF A DECOY

They encountered no more beasts in the depths of the Pulaski Forest, save the bears who lived in a town called Bear. The bears there seemed quite friendly, dressed in hoods and linen tunics and floppy hats. They lifted up their paws and waved as the van jolted through the main street of their log village, and the monks and kids all shouted, "Hi!" which was nice, though it confused Lily a little.

Lily had been thinking hard for the last few minutes, since they'd passed the bears' apiaries.* She watched bears in white coveralls and

_____

*An apiary is not a place where you keep apes. It is a place where you keep bees. If you keep apes there too, you'd better be ready to deal with one mad ape. And a thousand mad bees.

netted helmets drawing out honeycombs. Bees were trembling around them. Grzo waved and smiled a big, lopsided smile.

Lily was thinking about the concealment of monks. She was wondering why it was that Grzo wasn't more worried about being recognized. And what about the line of two hundred monks wandering through the wilderness on their way to their new home? What was happening to them?

"Brother Grzo?" she said.

"Yes, sweet girl?"

"How are the other monks going to make it

Of course, occasionally someone might try to keep both together. Someday you might meet someone like that.

I did, once. No, that was not a date I enjoyed.

It sounded nice, when the long sunset fell over the formal gardens of Chunderquist House, and the night-dew was falling on the nodding blooms and the scent of fresh-cut grass was in the air, and she said, "Would you like to see our apiary? Father keeps the sublimest hives." And so we wandered down through the marble patios and past the jonquils and the hollyhocks, and her brothers were playing badminton, and the evening was full of the linnet's wings as we rambled down to the bee-loud glade. Or ape-loud glade, as it turned out to be, and then the screaming, and the running, and the tearing, and me being strangulated, and *ouch! ouch! ouch!* . . . Well, you get the picture.

to the new Vbngoom? Won't they be kind of, I don't know, obvious, walking in a line like that?"

"Ah! But they shall walk most of the way through the wilderness, where there are no people to see them. And they know spells to cause angry persons to fall asleep, if all of them pray together. And most important, blessed child, we are a decoy."

Lily sat up straight. Jasper was looking startled, and Katie looked like she was suddenly on high alert, Code Red.

"So . . . ," said Lily, "by decoy . . . by decoy . . . you mean, like, we're providing a diversion?"

"Yes, yes!" Brother Grzo was very enthusiastic. "Very clever. We stop in each town and tell them where we are going. Soon every secret agent in northern Delaware will search for us on the road to Guyencourt—and no one will be looking in the mountains to the northwest."

"But we . . . ," said Lily. "We're not exactly

like a decoy. You know, like a duck decoy? It's made of wood. It's not a real duck."

"True. And to you I say: A decoy may be made of wood, but it still has eyes."

"But a decoy doesn't feel pain. And a decoy doesn't have feelings."

"And a decoy doesn't have hair," Katie added. "And a decoy doesn't have to go to the bathroom."

"And a decoy demands an explanation!" said Jasper. "How are we going to cross the border safely if the whole Ministry of Silence is looking for us?"

"Yes," said Brother Grzo. "This is a very good—quick, everyone wave!" He yelled out the window to some brown bears playing chess on a tavern porch, "OH, GREETINGS, GREETINGS, FINE CREATURES! YOU PAY US NO MIND! SIMPLY FOUR HUMBLE MONKS OF VBNGOOM AND THREE CHILDREN OF OTHER STATES HEADING FOR GUYENCOURT! NO

MATTER! GOOD DAY! FAREWELL!"

The van labored up a slope, coughing.

"You did not wave vigorously, blessed youths," he said. "But there is time. With the hours together, fellowship grows, and soon you will wish to spread your joy among all men and bears. What did we speak of?" There was no answer from the back. He looked into the rear-view mirror at the kids. They looked back at him. They looked a little grim. He said, "Well, no matter. Who wishes to sing, 'The Monks on the Bus Go Up and Down'? . . . Yes? . . . I begin?"

After that, the people in the van got much quieter.

Much quieter. *Much* quieter.

The people in the van got much quieter.

All through the town.

DINE AND DASH

The next afternoon they reached high Elsmere.

The van rattled out of a deep ravine with towering cliffs on each side to find, sparkling in front of them, the wings and blimps of the hovering city, home of the Zeppelin-Lords. The mansions and town houses of that place were suspended high, high in the stratosphere above the mountain, each held up by balloons or rotors or slowly flapping metal bat wings. Some of those homes had been aloft for centuries.

The green slopes of the mount were terraced into fields where the poor of the city labored. They staggered up and down the hillside with carts and baskets. Their rice paddies were shaded by the ungainly heli-burbs far above them.

Lily leaned over so she could see better out the front window. Katie, who had been napping, blinked groggily. Teenage Brother Bvletch also stared at the window, but he was checking out his reflection, scowling and stretching his cheeks to assess his blackheads.

"Elsmere," said Brother Grzo. "Here we must see a man in a restaurant."

"A man in a restaurant?" said Katie.

"A man with a plan."

"Like a menu?"

"A plan for our route."

"Don't we know our route?"

"We must hear from the man."

"But we know where we're going. We're going to the north."

"To the north or the south. To the east or the west."

"Even the south?" Jasper asked.

"That may be the plan."

"Says who?" said Katie.

"The man with the plan."

"What man with the plan?"

"The man in the restaurant."

"Why do I get the feeling," said Katie, "that I'm walking in circles even while I'm sitting in the same place?"

"Enlightenment?" Drgnan suggested cutely.

"I don't even get that."

"Are we not all walking in circles, even while we—"

"Okay, I think that's enough from monks for the moment," said Katie, holding up her hand. "No more from monks."

She and Drgnan began to wrestle. The seat twanged with their noogies.

They drove up the hill between terraced rice paddies.

When they reached the earthbound precincts of the city, Grzo parked.

Everyone got out. Lily stood for a moment and looked down the way they'd come, at all the tiny people laboring in the sun. The shadows of rotors and blimps passed over them. Lily did not feel good about it. She got the strong feeling that the Zeppelin-Lords and Copter-Barons and Gyro-Dukes above her would not have been able to sip cool drinks in their marble sky-palaces if it weren't for the people working in the muck a mile below them. It didn't seem very fair.

The others were already starting to walk up the steep street. She scurried along after them. There was a fence made of old pipes sunk into cement to stop people from plunging off the road.

The houses were built of concrete blocks and tin. They were overshadowed by huge billboards and scaffolds and gantries. There were a few older chalets among them, with ancient wood carving over the doors—whittled pinecones and holly sprigs and edelweiss. Donkey carts filled with rice bumped up the street.

The restaurant was a cracked stucco cube

hanging out over the city's retaining wall. It specialized in food for monks, and was called Friar Tuck-In.

Inside, it was smoky from burnt pods. There were big windows so customers could take in the view, but the glass was all streaked with greasy fingerprints.

Some of the customers were just regular people dressed in their work clothes, but there were also several other monks from other religious orders lounging around in robes of brown or gray, watching a prizefight on a little television.

Lily and her companions sat at a table. It rocked back and forth. Drgnan translated the laminated menu for the other kids. Most of the items on the menu were the kind of things monks ate—acorns, twigs, and locusts—but the restaurant also had hamburgers and "Bucky's World-Famous Fries," which Jasper was interested in. "It has been several days since I had a good meal," he said. "A man cannot live on beef jerky alone. I am thrilled for a side order."

"Oh," said Katie longingly. "You know what I could have? A Reuben. I love a Reuben sandwich. I can't wait."

Lily was famished. Even the smell of crispy grasshoppers made her belly rumble.

The waiter came to their table. He was dressed in a black robe and a grimy apron. He had a careful, secretive look to him. He began to speak in Doverian; Brother Grzo bowed his head and requested that the gentleman speak English for the benefit of the children.

The waiter nodded slowly. "Welcome to Friar Tuck-In," he said, with a Western twang. "I will be your waitstaff. It's a big, bruisin' pleasure to have you dine with us. You folks come a long way?"

"Yes," said Brother Grzo. "We are just coming up from the south."

The waiter nodded very slowly. "From the south. *Quite a trip.*" He looked into each of their faces with great significance.

"Quite a trip," agreed Grzo.

"Where are you folks headed?"

"Guyencourt," said Grzo. "All of us."

The waiter looked like he was filing the answer away for future reference. But all he said was, "Great. Happy trails. Can I interest you in the specials?"

"Yes," said Grzo. "Specials are full of hidden delight."

"For the monks among you, we got a bark sandwich with a homemade chipotle sauce served with chips and a side of gravel-and-spinach salad with a holy water vinaigrette dressing. For the rest of you, we got a fine ostrich stew, which comes with a side salad and hush puppies, exactly three deep-fried hush puppies, no more, no less. You got that?" he asked Brother Grzo.

"I do."

"I'd like the Reuben sandwich," said Katie. "Thanks so much." She put down her menu. "And a Coke."

"I'd like a hamburger and fries," said Jasper, "the meal of my homeland." He smiled winningly.

"You sure?" said the waiter.

"No," Grzo told the waiter. "Don't listen."

"But I *would* like a hamburger," said Jasper. "It's on the menu."

"And I'd like a hamburger too, please," said Lily.

Grzo said, "Please stop saying 'hamburger.'"

"But that's what I want," Jasper protested.

"Did you get my Reuben sandwich down?" Katie asked. "I love a Reuben."

The waiter's eyes were shocked and watching.

"Please, blessed children," said Brother Grzo, taking Lily and Jasper's hands in his own. He gave them a very wide, very loving, very lopsided smile. He leaned down close to the table and whispered, "The gentleman is speaking in code. Every item on the menu and the specials has a meaning."

"I see," said Jasper.

"If you keep on asking for hamburgers, fries, and Reubens, he will believe we are being pursued by lady musketeers. On zebra-back."

"Ohhhhh," said Katie. She picked up her menu. "Scratch the Reuben. No Reuben for me."

"What," said Brother Grzo, "would the gentleman recommend?"

The waiter answered, "Fish filet sandwich with cheddar cheese on a whole-wheat bun and a side of new potatoes and corn on the cob. Dessert, I think you monks'll enjoy our hemlock-berry pie with whipped cream and a scoop of briar ice cream."

Grzo thought long and hard about this. He gazed out the windows at the surrounding hills and peaks. Finally he nodded. "Please," said he. "That sounds delicious, my dear waiter. Pray place our order."

The waiter nodded, crossed out their order, and stuffed his pad in his pocket. He picked up Grzo's glass and poured the monk some water. He gave them all a warning look, wiped his hands on his apron, and went back to the kitchen.

Grzo was staring at his glass of water. He lifted it and turned it around.

There, in the mist on the glass, in the midst of Grzo's fingerprints, the waiter had drawn a letter Q.

Grzo frowned. He took a long drink from the glass, wiping off the Q with his thumb.

He looked around casually, then rose. "All right, blessed children," he said.

They looked at him in confusion. "What about lunch?" asked Katie.

"We have what we need," said Grzo. "We will pick it up *to go.*"

"We haven't ordered," said Katie.

"I ordered, sweet child."

"I mean what we want to eat."

"A Reuben sandwich will lead to great misunderstanding."

"What about a Coke?"

"He will believe you wish to buy a crossbow."

"This is impossible," said Katie. "Can't we order *anything*? Anything real?"

"Our order, shining light of youth, is *cooking now*. And the griddle is all too real, and all too hot. We fear burns." Grzo gestured toward the door. "Come along."

Unwillingly, they all filed back out onto the street. There was a kind of a traffic jam. A furniture salesman had put a bunch of tables and comfy reclining chairs out on the street for display. They were getting covered with dust and surrounded by sheep.

"Now, back to the van," said Grzo. "We have received our new instructions. We shall take an unusual detour, dear children."

Drgnan asked, "Where are we going, Brother?"

Grzo smiled and winked. "We shall go up in the air."

"Golly," said Jasper. "I'd been hoping!"

"We have laid our trail now," said Brother Grzo. "The Ministry of Silence believes we are headed for Guyencourt. But it is time for us to deceive. The pelican waves one wing to attract notice while he snatches fish with the other. We shall now be taken secretly up into the sky. They shall continue to look for us on the Montchanin Road—but we shall actually be in Wilmington."

"The old double-switch!" said Jasper, delighted.

"Is that true about the pelican?" said Katie. "I don't think they really use their wings to—"

"We shall fly like the starlings, darling children! Away from the cats who prowl by night! The waiter has just told me that all the preparations are being made."

"Why didn't you tell us about this switch yesterday, when you completely freaked us out by telling us we were a decoy?" asked Katie.

"I did not know until just now," said Grzo. "I had to be kept in ignorance."

"But you're in charge of everything!" said Katie.

"You know that the monks of Vbngoom cannot lie. We have taken an oath of truth. So if I had known we were not really going to Guyencourt, I could not have yelled out the window that we were headed there. I would have had to yell, 'Greetings, fine citizens! We four monks and three out-of-state children are pretending to go to Guyencourt, but actually are going to be lifted into the sky in Elsmere to be delivered to Wilmington!' This would not have been a wise deception."

"So you had to be fooled yourself," Lily asked, "in order to fool others?"

"There is sometimes a virtue in not-knowing."

With that, they began walking through the sheep back toward their van.

They left the furniture behind them.

One of the reclining chairs folded up its footrest, stood, and watched them go.

It was Mrglik, Delaware's greatest furniture-imitating spy.

He and Bntno had been driving down the Montchanin Road for a couple of days, looking for the van. When they reached Elsmere, they split up, and Mrglik, always eager for practice, had spent his lunch hour at the furniture store being a vanity and a comfortable reclining chair.

He had heard everything.

He pulled out his gun. "Stop!" he cried. "You—monks—kids—*STOP! YOU'RE UNDER ARREST!*"

Rice and Danger!

Of course, Jasper, Katie, and Lily heard only something that they didn't understand yelled in Doverian. But Grzo swooped his arms around them from behind and rushed them forward, head bowed.

"What's wrong?" said Katie.

"Run, children," said Grzo. "We all must run for the van. Very fast."

Mrglik stood behind them on the sheep-filled street, pointing his .38. He ordered, "Stop!" again in Doverian—and when that didn't work, started shouting in English, "BOY! GIRL! STOP!"

"Who is that?" said Katie.

"YOU IS BENEATH THE ARREST!"

Lily took a quick look back. "It's Mrglik!" she said. "Last week he disguised himself as a bed in our hotel room!"

"And a nightstand," said Katie venomously.

"STOP OR I TO SHOOT!"

"Run, blessed children!" said Grzo. "Quick and light as angels' wings!"

Then the bullets started flitting past them.

Bvletch had already reached the van and yanked the door open, holding out his hand to help the others in, while keeping up a steady stream of sarcasm, according to his vow. ("Oh, wow, this is great. My soul sings like the frog in spring. How did you know what I wanted for my birthday?")

Grzo was no longer behind Lily, but in front of her, holding out his hand to grab hers as they both charged toward the van. Their fingers missed—she was falling back. The bullets kept flying. None of them hit anything.

Mrglik was running down toward them now, forcing his way between the protesting sheep. He fired again, and his bullet shattered one of the van's windows. Everyone ducked.

Lily was hiding behind a rice cart, stooped down so she couldn't be hit. But she was still fifteen feet or so away from the van and her friends.

Grzo crouched near the wheels of his ride, extending his arm toward her, whispering, "Lily. Come. Slither." By his side, Drgnan watched her, tense.

She was terrified. She couldn't tell where Mrglik was. She didn't want to raise her head up over the top of the cart.

She knew that Mrglik didn't really want to kill anyone. He needed to take them alive if he wanted to get information from them. But she had heard that the Ministry of Silence was brutal, and she didn't want to take any chances. She pressed her face against the wood of the cart and shut her eyes. She wished it would all go away.

But instead she heard another shot fired—and heard it strike the dirt by her feet.

How—?!?

Mrglik was leaning down, firing under the cart. He smiled at her under the cart and waved.

"Come out," he said, "and you not will be harmed."

Startled, sick with fear, she grabbed the rim of the cart and pulled her legs up off the ground. She clutched herself close to the planks. Her arm was thrown over the lip now, and her hand was buried in rice pilaf.

She heard Mrglik approaching. Soft soles on dust.

"Lily!" Drgnan urged.

Step by step, Mrglik got closer.

She could practically feel him stretching out his arm to reach over the corner of the cart and take ahold of her. . . .

But then the cart began to move backward. Her slight weight had started it rolling.

She was hanging on to the downhill side of it. It didn't have any brakes. So, slowly at first, it began creaking down the switchback road with Lily gripping the lip for dear life.

She screamed and looked up. Mrglik was running along behind, his gun in his hand.

Drgnan was pounding along beside her and the cart, his robes flashing around him.

She heard Mrglik shouting fiercely in his own language.

There was a shudder—the whole cart tipped—righted itself—rolled on.

Now with Drgnan aboard.

Drgnan reached over the side and pulled Lily in.

She tumbled over the side, scraping her belly on the wood.

She and Drgnan were a-sift in a deep pool of dry rice. The cart was hurtling now, the hill steep and the road rough. Mrglik flung himself along behind, grabbing at the traces and shafts.

He put his hand on the cart. Drgnan brought his fist down on it, and Mrglik pulled back his arm, cursing. He shoved the gun back in its holster.

The spy reached out. He clamped both hands to the cart—which slowed with the drag. Soon he would have them stalled. Lily began prying at his fingers. She pried one, then Drgnan another, then Lily, then Drgnan. They took turns—like a lover plucking off flower petals and saying, "She loves me not."

Mrglik dropped back, unhanded—but still armed. He pulled out the pistol again.

Then he flung himself bodily—and landed half on the pile of rice, with half his body still dragging on the ground. His legs wheeled wildly as he tried to get his knee up on the cart shaft.

Drgnan grabbed him and they went into a fearsome clinch. Mrglik kicked hard with both legs and bucked himself all the way into the cart, while Drgnan tried to pry away the man's gun.

Lily looked down the street and saw the cart was careening toward a stone wall. They were going to smash—and die in a flurry of rice pilaf new-plucked from the pilaf fields below.

Drgnan grimaced with effort as the man in his black suit and cushions (I perhaps should have mentioned that Mrglik was still wearing some of the cushions from pretending to be a chair) writhed and tried to point his gun, all the while yelling, "HALT!" as if anyone could halt the rumbling, tumbling, hazardous progress of that rickety cart as it swooped toward the wall and certain—

But no! Lily had her hand on one of the traces, and she was yanking it as hard as she could!

The cart turned! Spun out a little, sending a flurry of rice off the side, but missing the wall by inches!

She could control the wheels, she realized. She fished for the other trace.

Got it. Now she looked behind her, the two leather straps in her hands. The cart was still rolling backward down the road.

Toward some little kids, standing in the road and looking wonderingly up at the fight.

The cart would plow right through them. They all wore their paper smiley-face masks, the uniform of schoolkids in the Autarch's dictatorship.

Whizz—Lily yanked and just missed them.

Jiggle—headed right toward a baby in a carriage! The baby looked at the hurtling cart and plucked at its mouth with a chubby finger.

Lily clenched and pulled. Turned just in time. The baby carriage tottered with the wind of passage.

A mother cat! And kittens! Twelve of them! In the road! Cute as buttons!

Lily tugged the trace with all her might. The rice sifted—shifted—spilled over the shafts! And the cart missed the kits.

A perfect daisy! Growing up through the road! Bringing sunshine and happiness to everyone who passed it on the way to their rice fields!

Lily caromed the cart off the curb and the flower just shivered with the spin of the spokes.

Honking! From where?

The van! Riding alongside them! At the same speed!

Cobbles rattled beneath the wheels. The door was open. Jasper and Bvletch reached out to receive whoever wanted to try to jump the gap between the vehicles.

Lily couldn't leave the traces or Drgnan would be stuck in the hurtling cart with no control over the wheels.

"Go!" said Drgnan, fighting Mrglik.

The gun dropped from Mrglik's hand. Lily saw it slide into the rice. She reached for it, but the cart tipped.

"Go!" yelled Drgnan again.

Lily leaped—was grabbed by her friends and pulled into the van.

"We have to help Drgnan!" she said.

"Look who's behind us," said Katie.

Lily looked back—and saw their old guide, Bntno, driving a little car behind them. He was yelling out the window in English, "Hasty children! Do not run away! Come sit with Bntno in his excellent little car!"

That was what was behind them. And in front of them? Lily looked forward—and saw that both the van and the cart were headed for a low concrete wall where the switchback road turned. The van could turn. But Drgnan had to get out of the cart in the next few seconds—or he'd be over the wall and falling freely, showered with rice—like a wedding and a funeral all at once.

DEAD END ALLEY

Van and cart raced for the wall.

They had to both swerve, or they'd be flipping off the edge of a cliff.

Behind them was Bntno, a new danger. Lily didn't know what to do. Jasper was clearly contemplating jumping into the rice to help his friend—but that would mean certain death when the cart hit.

Drgnan looked up from his wrestling. Saw the wall.

He struggled to get free—but Mrglik had a grip on him. . . . Drgnan couldn't . . . pull himself . . . away. . . .

Unless . . .

THWAM!

They hit the wall.

The cart flew up into the air.

Drgnan scissored his legs—spun. He rose above the cart like a saint ascending, his arms spread wide, a halo of rice pilaf glittering around him.

He landed on the roof of the van, spread-eagled.

The cart and Mrglik were tumbling down the hillside. Mrglik could be heard yelling ouches. His cushions were little comfort now.

The door to the van was still open. Jasper hung out of it, yelling up at Drgnan to see if he was okay.

Drgnan's shaved head popped down from the roof. "What does a side of rice pilaf mean in the code of Friar Tuck-In?" he asked. "Because for me, it means victory."

Katie looked at him adoringly.

He scrambled down with Jasper and Bvletch's help.

Now they were all in the van and only had

to deal with the problem of Bntno. Except Bntno was on a cell phone, probably calling the secret police.

Katie and Lily dragged the van's door shut.

They screeched into a side alley. Bntno shot past.

"Huzzah!" cheered Jasper.

But at the next alley, Bntno roared out from a side road.

The chase was still on.

There were sirens.

The van roared down an avenue plastered on either side with billboards advertising beer and milk and hamburger sandwiches.

Two secret police cars rolled out behind them and joined the chase.

Lily started to think about what Grzo had mentioned to them regarding dungeons where they might be kept if they were caught: the darkness . . . the toads . . . the slime to drink . . . questions being asked about where the monks and their monastery were hidden. . . . She wanted desperately to be at home, to be lying on her bed with a book, with her mom and dad cooking dinner in the kitchen. . . .

She shut her eyes, as if that would somehow wake her from a bad dream.

She opened them, and of course nothing had changed.

The van crossed a bridge over a deep crevasse. Children swayed on balloon harnesses, hovering by the cliffs.

Now they were back in tricky little streets, shuddering along elevated roads that swerved and wobbled like old roller coaster tracks supported by scaffolds of wood. Shacks were caught in the scaffolds like flies in a web.

Bntno bobbed up and down after the van. He was yelling something out the window, but nobody could hear. The secret police were right behind him.

"Does anyone want the radio on?" asked Brother Grzo's monk copilot from the driver's seat. "I do not mean that we should be silent."

Nobody answered him.

Brother Grzo frowned at the road.

Behind them, Bntno was urging on the secret police. Their sirens were wailing and they pulled ahead of him. Their windows rolled down. Arms came out holding pistols.

They were firing at the van.

Everyone was screaming along through some kind of dock land now. Blimps were rising and falling around them. Six-armed dockworkers drove forklifts in muddy yards.

Hit!

The van was hit! The tire popped with a smack!

The van began to rattle, agitated. *Clunk*—wobbling—one tire flat! The rim biting rubber!

Screeched around a corner—the cops after them—

The van shot through a gate.

Lily saw it was a dead end.

The gate slammed shut behind them.

Outside, the cops pulled up by the shut gate, waited.

Bntno roared past, squealed to a stop. He pulled back.

"They're in there," said one of the secret police. "They can't go anywhere. It's a dead end. We've got them."

"Let's knock down the door," said another.

It took them only a few minutes to commandeer a forklift.

Then they ran it repeatedly into the gate.

Eventually, the gate fell down.

And they confronted . . . nothing.

An empty little alley leading nowhere.

As if the van had vanished.

"Huh?" said the secret police.

"Wha?"

"Whoa."

"Wow."

"Where?"

And far above, dangling from a hook, the people in the van looked down on the scene as they were lifted into the sky—into a cargo hold—peering down through thin vapor to the tiny cars, the little spies—seeing the law of the dictator dwindle beneath them.

A Rendezvous with Agent Q

The sky freighter's first mate took good care of them. He bustled them out of the van, once it was locked in the hold, and ushered them up a ladder to the lounge. He showed them to chairs. He offered them tea and made them popcorn in a battered old microwave that was surrounded by wrenches, screwdrivers, stale donuts, and a grimy calendar showing the tusked, six-armed women of Lumbrook sprawled out on glaciers, dressed in bikinis.

The freighter's name was the *Snow-Bow*, and she was a fine little ship. She looked like a seashell supported by parachutes. The parachutes were constantly filled with air by rows of thick, trumpety pipes that sprouted out of the bottom of the ship and twisted upward. They constantly blew tempest winds up into the 'chutes, keeping the freighter suspended.

Jasper was fascinated by this method of propulsion. "By Jove," he said, "it's like lifting yourself by the seat of your own pants." So with Drgnan translating, he got a tour of the engine room from the first mate. When they'd examined the giant hair-dryer technology that made flight possible, Drgnan and Jasper scampered up and down the length of the vessel, exploring, pointing out the windows at the cities below and above.

The secret police had dispatched a helicopter to look for the flying van. By the time they started patrolling the skies, however, shining their searchlight into windows, the freighter had mingled with others like it, swinging around in circles, a complicated dance of bees, until it was impossible to tell which freighter concealed the van and the monks.

Grzo talked gently as they all gazed out the windows at the hovering spires above them.

"The crew on this heavenly ship, dear children, are all members of the Delaware Resistance Movement, devoted to removing the Awful and Adorable Autarch from power and restoring our rightfully elected Governor."

"Where's the Governor?" asked Lily.

"None know," said Grzo. "Not for many years. Not since the Autarch took power. The Governor may have escaped the palace safely or—the gods forbid it!—the Governor may be imprisoned even now in Fort Delaware, off the coast."

"So where are we going now?" asked Jasper.

"We go to Wilmington. There we shall stay in a safe house secretly owned by the Resistance. There we shall await a secret agent sent by Washington, DC, who shall help us cross the border into the other United States. We must be very careful—for with the spying of your acquaintance Mrglik, the Ministry of Silence may now know that we do not head for Guyencourt, as we claimed."

"A spy?" said Jasper. "From Washington, DC? Golly, that's swell. Will he have gadgets?"

"I do not know," said Brother Grzo. "Like a handheld back massager?"

"Like an amphibious car. That goes on land and underwater and through lava."

Grzo admitted, "I know nothing of this agent."

"What?" said Katie. "Wait a second. You at least know his real name or something."

"No, child."

"Or a password. Or a sign to put in a window. Like one lantern if by land, two if by sea. You must know something."

"The waiter at Friar Tuck-In could not tell me, even in code, who the agent is. I know only that he shall meet us . . . and that he is called Agent Q."

"Agent Q," grumbled Katie. "That's not a name. That's a bathroom tile cleaner."

Grzo folded his hands before him. "The waiter drew a Q with his finger on the frost of my water glass. This was his sign to me."

"That's all he could say? 'Q'? Nothing else?"

"No, child."

"No real name?"

"No."

"And we don't know what the guy looks like?"

"Or that the agent we shall meet is, as the lively child says, 'a guy.' All of us who are monks must be kept in a state of ignorance, because we have taken the vow never to lie, even to our enemies. Knowledge is dangerous for us. We must remain blank."

"So you're the head of this expedition," said Katie, "and you don't even know how we're supposed to find the spy who's going to bring us across the border?"

"That is correct."

"You're just going to *wait* and hope this spy finds us?"

"Do not fear, sweet nettled one. The spy who seeks us shall be as subtle as the serpent and as quick as the hawk."

"This is so stupid!"

"You are touched by wrath, child of Pelt."

Katie sputtered, "Okay, I'm not touched—no, I'm not . . . I'm just . . . This is not a good way to run an adventure."

Lily, for a minute, was a little embarrassed that Katie was being so rude. But then Katie said what Lily herself was thinking: "Brother Grzo, I mean, I'm sorry, but do you know how long it's been since I've seen my parents? It's been days. They don't even know where we are. I lied to them and said we were going to sleep overnight inside one of Jasper's rockets for a science project. Eating stuff out of tubes." She shook her head. "I'm sorry to be kind of a brat," she said, "but we need to get home. They'll be worried about us."

Brother Grzo took Katie's hands in his own and he said, "Dear child, you are no brat. You are anxious and afraid. And who could not understand that? Even the shark sheds tears when it is away from its mother."

"Um . . . are you sure?"

"The shark is a very moody creature."

"But I mean, about the crying. 'Cause the shark is underwater? So how could you tell, like, when it . . ." Katie realized that she was supposed to be apologizing, not poking holes in Grzo's metaphors. She stopped herself, considered, and said, "I guess the sea is one big, salty tear."

Brother Grzo smiled his huge, lopsided smile. "Now you speak truth," said he. He lifted up her hands before him, and insisted, "Do not fear. The day after tomorrow, you shall be reunited with your family."

"You promise?" said Katie, warily. "You can't lie, remember."

"Yes, child, I promise you shall see them," said Grzo, nodding consolingly. Then he added: "Either on Earth, or in Heaven."

Which was not a very comforting thing to add.

While the freighter waited for clearance to leave Elsmere, Drgnan, Bvletch, and Jasper listened to entertaining stories told by the first mate, Dnny. He was six-armed, tusked, friendly, and unshaven. He wore jeans and a bandanna tied around his head. He was telling them a great story about his previous rig, a little ship he flew by himself called the *Hornet Mistress*. He spoke no English, so Drgnan translated for Jasper. It was a thrilling story, full of shootouts with the secret police, near escapes in the Newark Mountains, and a crash in the desert east of Sandtown.

The story ended this way: After many trials and tribulations, Dnny's little ship had finally reached the end of her run in Winterthur, north of Elsmere—a town where the pines and firs are crystalline with ice all year round, high up on the cliffs above the Montchanin Valley.

"He says," Drgnan reported, "that after the battle he reached the docks of Winterthur . . . and stumbled out of the ship's cockpit . . . smoking and covered in laser burns. . . . The ship never flew again."

"That's a pity which could make a robot weep," Jasper lamented. "Why didn't she fly again? The lasers had burst her balloons?"

"No," Drgnan said. "When he got out of the ship alive . . . he kissed the ship in thanks for her service to him . . . for getting him through safely."

"Ah," exclaimed Jasper, rapt, "for she was 'yare'!"

Drgnan listened to Dnny for a minute, nodding sympathetically. "He says," Drgnan explained, "that it is not a good idea for a man with tusks to kiss a helium balloon he loves."

"Oh," said Jasper.

"Yes," said Drgnan sadly. "He tells me there was a loud *pop*—which, brother, was no more resounding than the *pop* of his breaking heart. The balloon burst. And then his ship shot up into the air, over to the side, over to the other side, and *boom*. She fell down to the bottom of the cliffs. He cried her name . . . squeakily . . . in a really high-pitched voice . . . because of the helium." Drgnan shook his head. "It was not an easy time for him."

Dnny was looking out sadly at the night sky.

"So then," said Drgnan, "he joined the crew of this ship, the *Snow-Bow*. He's been sailing with them ever since."

As if the freighter had heard her name being called, there was a jolt.

Her engines had picked up. Outside, the lights of Elsmere began to shift and pass. The *Snow-Bow* had started her voyage through the night sky toward Wilmington and whatever dangers lay there.

As the ship rose, Lily and Katie sat side by side on the row of stained chairs that looked out over the benighted city.

The two girls gazed out at the spindles and arches of light cast by the flying palaces. It was beautiful to watch the half-seen structures rise and rotate. In the darkness, the festive airborne town was like a whole mythology of constellations come to Earth to celebrate some holiday or great conjunction: Gemini, the Twins, bringing two pizzas, one veggie, one meat; Capricorn donating a cheesecake; Aquarius carrying a vat of ginger-ale punch served by the Big Dipper; and Cancer, the Crab, with Pisces, the Fish, whispering over in the corner, worried they'll encounter seafood dip near the chips.

Um, that was kind of a long simile. All I'm really saying is that the lights were pretty.

After a long silence, Katie said to her friend, "You're lucky. You got to fight in the same pile of rice as Drgnan."

Lily was a little confused. "I'm not really sure I'd call it 'lucky.'"

"You got to have bullets shot at you, and he was all worried about you."

"It, you know, it wasn't so great, Katie. The bullets."

"Okay. So maybe the bullets weren't the best thing, but you have to admit, you got to beat up Mrglik together. That was fun, wasn't it?"

"No," said Lily. "Not really."

"How could beating up a spy not be fun with Drgnan?"

"It's nothing against Drgnan. If I have to beat up a spy with anyone, it would—"

"I know. It was probably scary. But I'm jealous that you got to fight in the same rice cart as him. I guess that's what I'm saying. I wish it was me in the rice cart."

"Maybe," said Lily hopefully, "maybe you'll get shot at with him the next time."

She heard what she had just said, and she couldn't help smiling to herself.

Katie saw her smile.

"Thanks," said Katie sarcastically. "Thanks for wishing the big wish: Me. Drgnan. Gunplay."

The two girls grinned, then started laughing. The dark hills swayed beneath them, and the ship rose toward the sky.

Don't you love it, in books, when wishes come true?

THE WASTELAND

For breakfast they had microwave sausage and microwave pancakes. The ship's captain even lent them some of his syrup. Everyone ate looking out over the landscape.

They had just passed to the north of Mount Minquadale. Now they were flying over huge gouges in the hills, and gray, smoldering slag heaps. There were cranes on the roads, and the rivers ran black.

Lily had the same feeling she'd had when she saw the people struggling up to the lower city of Elsmere from their rice paddies: the feeling that not everything was wonderful in this mythical country.

"What is all that down there?" she asked.

"The Brandywine Hills," said Brother Grzo sadly. "It is one of the most beautiful places in all of Delaware. Ah, that is to say, it was. (Sorrow take me.) Once, it was beautiful. Lakes and forests. The little towns of Arden and Claymont. Bobcats and pheasants. But now the lakes are thick with brown grime and the forests are chopped down to stumps and the hills are stripped for mining."

"By who?" asked Katie, aghast.

"The Governing Committee of Wilmington. They rule all you see beneath us. They are powerful men and women, friends and business partners of the Autarch. They make their fortunes by plundering the hills. They serve the Autarch. They do not care if this land is despoiled. They never leave Wilmington Castle. There they sit, reaping the profit of this smoky harvest."

"That's awful," said Lily.

"Alas, who are we to complain?" Grzo mused. "We too wish to have our roads, our van, our metal beds and lamps and flying ships. Where shall these metals come from, or the timbers for our houses?" He gestured with his hand to the rubble of the hills below them. "What we ask for must come from places like this."

"It is true about us wanting our flying ships," said Jasper ruefully. "Flying ships are extremely keen."

Columns of smoke rose past the windows.

After breakfast, they all went down to the freighter's hold, where they spray-painted the van red. It was extremely satisfying. Lily loved watching the white disappear in stripes and strokes. Katie, Drgnan, and Jasper loved threatening to color each other's hair. Katie shrieked and ducked. Drgnan pointed out that he didn't have any hair. Jasper said he'd paint some in, and Katie said she'd give him a center part.

Lily wondered why she was always too timid to join in when the others knocked each other around. It looked fun. But she felt more like someone who watched than someone who joined in.

By the time they had finished with the first coat of paint and gone above-decks for lunch, the airship had reached the outskirts of Wilmington. Its factories and housing blocks lay as far as the eye could see. Trains moved sluggishly on tracks.

Very little of the old city of Wilmington survived. Though there were a few enclaves where the houses were made of stone and the streets were quaint and narrow, most of the city was now a great industrial center. The most prominent reminder of the city's past, that age of fable when the purple-sailed ships of Wilmington plied all the trade routes of Delaware Bay, their navy bringing fear even to the savage barbarians of Broadkill, Slaughter Beach, and Hazzard Landing, was the castle that still stood on a rocky hill above the city, commanding a view of all the tenements, mills, and chemical vats for miles around.

Jasper, Katie, Lily, and Drgnan looked

down at Wilmington Castle. Immediately they hated it. Its battlements and conical roofs were black with soot. Something about its jagged turrets spelled doom.

If only they had known what dire interrogations were about to happen there.

CRAZY HAY

In ten minutes or so, the freighter anchored at an air dock. The hair-dryer blasts that held the ship aloft gradually diminished from high to medium. A winch cranked in the anchor cable, pulling the ground upward toward the *Snow-Bow.*

The ship landed gently on a wide sheet-metal platform scored with rocket blasts and acid burns. Men ran out to secure the freighter with chains.

Grzo came into the ship's lounge to watch the preparations with the kids. He was dressed in khaki pants about an inch too short, old running shoes, and a T-shirt that said,

I SURVIVED THE FIFTH ANNUAL ELLENDALE OFFICE SUPPLIES BONANZA! FEBRUARY 1989!!

"Disguise," he explained.

Katie asked, "Where did you get the shirt? I mean . . . *where?*"

"The monastery rummage sale, child. We must hide our monkishness under a bushel. Or behind a veil. The Ministry of Silence knows to seek seven persons in a white van—four monks, three children from out of the state. So we must deceive them. We shall dress like people of the world and shall travel separately to the safe house. You four shall walk with Bvletch. Bvletch shall guide you. Us two, the adults, shall go to a garage and finish disguising the van. This coat of paint is nearly dry. We shall fix the window and add a sign on the doors to further mislead the border police. Then we shall join you at the safe house, most likely on the morrow, when the new morn breaks over the radar dishes of the east." He handed parcels to Drgnan and Bvletch. "Your costumes," he said.

Drgnan bowed. "I render thanks for the disguise that shall preserve me."

Bvletch unfolded his parcel and looked down at his new clothes. "What," he said, "you've entered me for Prom King at the Dork Ball?"

Grzo said gently, "They are such clothes as fine people of leisure wear when vacationing in seaside towns to ease their troubled minds and refresh vexed spirits."

Bvletch pulled out a pair of green shorts with a repeated whale and cocker spaniel pattern on them. "It's never too late to get beat up on the playground," he said.

Katie said, "Wow. Whales. That brings back memories."

Bvletch protested, "Even the starlings will mock me."

"Away with you," said Grzo lovingly. "Change. Return. You shall not be recognized."

In a minute Bvletch and Drgnan came out of their cabin dressed in their new togs. Bvletch wore the spaniel-and-whale shorts and an Izod shirt with the collar up. Drgnan was dressed in plaid shorts, flip-flops, and a Tyrant Splash T-shirt (THE GREAT TASTE OF DELAWARE!).

Lily watched Katie's eyes widen. As much as Katie had thought Drgnan was dreamy-esque in monastic robes, she clearly thought he was even more dreamy-esque in an old cotton tee.

Drgnan saw her staring. "How do I look?" he asked.

"Great," said Katie. "I mean . . . yeah . . . great."

"What matters is not how you look," Grzo cautioned. "Appearances are but shadows."

"Fine for my renowned master to say," grumbled Bvletch, slipping on his penny loafers. "He isn't wearing embroidery whales."

Brother Grzo gave them instructions on how to get to the town's main market. "Once there, find a fishery called Wilt's. Go into Wilt's and ask for table seventeen, by the bay. They shall lead you to the safe house. Be alert. No one must know where you go or from whence you come."

The kids repeated the instructions back. They bid a fond farewell to the captain of the *Snow-Bow* and to Dnny. They said good-bye to the two adult monks.

Grzo embraced each of them. "I shall see you tomorrow. I hope that by this time, the spy shall have made himself known, and we shall set off either on the ferry or across the border just north of here. By tomorrow evening, my children, lights of my soul, we shall be in the state of New Jersey. Is that not cause for rejoicing?"

"It'll be nice to get home," said Katie. "Our parents must be really worried. Thank you for everything you're doing to get us back to them."

Grzo bowed. "I do nothing. I, too, eagerly anticipate the day that I can return home to my Scriptorium in Vbngoom and take up my quills again. The swamp rat, washed to sea, longs for its own special burrow." He smiled sadly.

Soon the five kids were shown out of a hidden door. They walked through the docks, past crates and pallets and cranes, and made their way through the great thoroughfares of Wilmington.

Everywhere there was suspicion in the air. People looked both ways before stepping out of their front doors. Men in long coats whispered to one another. Figures stood on old, baroque bridges, pretending to watch birds with binoculars. A fishmonger watched two old women in head scarves pass, then muttered a report into the mouth of a trout.

"I wonder how the spy from Washington, DC, shall possibly find us," said Jasper, peering around and adjusting his pith helmet. "And how will we know him when he appears?"

"We must be as watchful as falcons," said Drgnan. He looked suspiciously at a dachshund.

A little girl hopscotching on the pavement stopped one-legged near six, goggled, smiled a big, toothless smile, and said, "Hello!"

Katie smiled and said, "Hello, there!" back.

This was a mistake.

Once they had passed, the little girl watched them for a minute, then spat some chewing tobacco on the pavement. She slowly put her other leg down and went over to make a telephone call.

"Five of them," she said in Doverian. "I heard them. They were talking English. They're not from around here." The voice on the other end asked her something. She answered, "Yup. . . .

Yup. . . . Nope. No monks. They were mostly in shorts. But two of them didn't have hair. . . . Yup. . . . Yeah. . . . Ummmm, I want Z-347. The Precious Moments figurines. . . . Either 'You're My Sunshine' or 'Best Friends Are Forever.' . . . Okay. And I haven't gotten the hockey stick I ordered for turning in Mrs. Lpnzski. What are you people running, a secret police or a pizza party? Get on it—*pronto!*"

The five friends walked briskly through the streets, seeking Wilt's Fishery. They were in one of the few old sections of town. The streets, though they had once been painted bright colors, were now dark and grim. The old plaster of the crumbling rococo facades was cracked and blackened. Streaks of grime ran down from windows that had once been grand.

Many of the oldest houses were built around courtyards, with few windows at all on the outside—just huge, carved doors. It was as if even the architecture didn't trust people, and turned inward rather than showing things freely on its face.

Bvletch led them along watchfully. He no longer acted sour and sarcastic. He had dropped all pretense of irony. He clearly knew he was responsible for their safety, and he took no chances. He was careful to look nonchalant, but at the same time, his eyes were shifting around to notice whether anyone was following.

When disaster struck, however, there was little he—or anyone else—could do.

The five were walking down a narrow old street when a truck bumbled along behind them. The bales of hay on the back were stacked precariously, preposterously, leaning out over the sides. The driver couldn't get past the kids. He honked.

They flattened themselves against the wall. The truck inched forward.

When it was beside them, it idled. The engine puttered. Diesel smoke drifted around them.

"Watch," said Bvletch. He clearly didn't like what was going on.

Lily and Katie tried to sidle backward so they weren't trapped.

Drgnan and Jasper waited patiently.

Then bales of hay slid out from the stack— pushed from within. They tumbled into the gutter. And hands shot out to grab the kids.

"Great time to stay where you are!" shouted Bvletch, which was his way of suggesting they run.

Jasper and Drgnan struggled with the hands. Katie and Lily pulled themselves backward, stumbling out behind the truck.

The hands fumbled with our heroes' elbows. They held out torn pieces of cloth. At first Jasper assumed they were to bind his arms—but then he realized, "Chloroform! They're trying to knock us out!"

He reached up, grabbed a block of hay, and yanked it violently down. It struck two of the spies on the head, and they collapsed forward—

just as Drgnan leaped up, striking their foreheads with his knees and knocking them silly.

Three hands had clamped onto Bvletch. A fourth hand passed a chloroform-soaked rag to a fifth hand. The fifth hand moved it toward Bvletch's mouth, which was raving, "This is great. You're the best hay I've ever met. Wow, you guys are my favorite crop. My spirit lights up like—ow—*ow!*"

Katie and Lily looked around them to see if there was any way they could help. Jasper and Drgnan were tangling with their spies. Bvletch was being dragged toward the holes in the hay.

"Bvletch!" Katie shouted in alarm—not so much to get his attention as to point out his predicament to Drgnan. She pointed and screamed, "No! Look! Bvletch!"

Drgnan turned and saw his fellow monk being lifted into the thatch. He delivered a final swipe and wriggled along the stone wall to try to catch hold of Bvletch's penny loafers before they disappeared forever.

Then the hands grabbed Drgnan himself.

And Jasper found himself overwhelmed.

There were too many of them in the truck.

The girls were panicked. They plunged back toward their friends, plucking at baling wire and trying to topple the straw.

There's no way we can fight this many adults, Lily thought in terror. Jasper was beating at a hand that clenched a rag against his nose and cheek—but he was clearly getting weaker.

Lily saw Jasper and Drgnan lifted off their feet, both of them reeling with fumes. They were about to be pulled inside.

And as they hung there, suspended in the arms of their abductors, the truck began to drive away.

HAYRIDE OF HATE

"*Stop! Halt!*" somebody yelled in English.

The arms in the hay paid no attention.

"I said, *Stop!*" the voice repeated.

Now the arms slowed down for a second.

Drgnan and Jasper, struggling faintly, both hung with their shoes dabbling in the gutter. Their heads rolled on their shoulders.

Bvletch was already gone, disappeared into the fodder.

The new speaker was a boy, perhaps about fifteen—older than Lily and Katie. He had a stern, commanding face and excellent hair for stunts. Instead of a weapon, he held in front of him a Megaluxe Game Wedge™.

"Taylor Quizmo, Secret Agent!" the boy

announced. Then he waved the Game Wedge™ and ordered, "Stop where you are!"

A guy leaned from the passenger-side window and pointed out, "That is a video game. A child's toy. Not a weapon."

"Think again, friend," said Taylor Quizmo, Secret Agent. "Taylor Quizmo doesn't play games." He pressed a hidden button, and a spray of green sleeping gas poured out of the pointy part of the Wedge.

"Back! Back!" voices in the hay shouted to the driver. The driver hit the clutch and jolted the truck into reverse.

Lily and Katie threw themselves against the wall so they wouldn't get squooshed. "Grab them!" Lily shouted, which doesn't make much sense when I write it, but did make sense when she shouted it—because the half-conscious Drgnan and Jasper were sliding by. The arms in the hay had gotten a taste of their own sleeping medicine—they drooped—and it wasn't hard for Katie and Lily to start a little tug-of-war with their friends as ropes.

Meanwhile, Taylor Quizmo, Secret Agent, was running toward the truck, spraying his aerosol sleeping gas and looking stern.

"Bvletch!" Lily yelled to him, and Katie joined her: "They've still got Bvletch!"

"Who's . . . ?" Taylor Quizmo asked.

"A friend! In the hay!" Lily yelled.

Taylor Quizmo looked around, a little confused. He had just run into his own cloud of sleeping gas.

The truck kept rolling.

Lily and Katie held on to their friends for dear life.

Drgnan and Jasper collapsed like sacks into the girls' arms.

The truck—with Bvletch still somewhere in it—screeched backward as the street got wider. It turned around and tore off.

Katie was leaning over Drgnan, slapping him. Jasper was blinking and sitting up. Taylor Quizmo was struggling to keep awake.

Everyone else was busy. So Lily ran after the truck.

It pulled out into a main street. It started honking wildly. It didn't move. Half-gutted lumps of hay rolled off into the street. A struggle of spy arms and legs was visible in the mound of feed.

Lily realized why it wasn't moving: The driver had fallen asleep. His head was bobbing on the horn.

That might buy us time, she thought, puffing toward the cab of the truck. She hoped she could pull Bvletch out of the mess.

The driver had fallen asleep—but the spy in the passenger seat had not. He pressed the driver's leg down. The leg pressed the foot. The foot pressed the pedal. And the pedal set the whole mechanism of internal combustion rolling.

The truck sped off, swerving, up the hill toward the Castle on its forbidding peak. It took off with Bvletch still inside.

The alley behind it was left strewn with dazed bodies.

TABLE FOR FIVE

"He's gone," said Lily, pale with horror. "They got him. They took him toward the Castle."

The others were starting to stand, looking groggy and unsteady.

"Who's missing?" asked Taylor Quizmo, Secret Agent. "One of the monks?"

"Brother Bvletch," answered Drgnan.

"We've got to go after him," said Katie. She was giving Jasper a hand with his backpack.

"No," said Taylor Quizmo. "Let's get you to the safe house. There we can talk to agents for the Resistance. They have people inside the Castle. We can make a plan with them." He looked carefully at Katie. "Can I help you up?" he asked.

She checked her legs. "It's too late," she said. "I'm already standing."

"It's never too late to help a beautiful lady to her feet." He gave her a quick, boyish wink and said to everyone, "Let's go. We want to move fast."

"This way," said Drgnan.

As they walked, they all introduced themselves.

Taylor Quizmo had a shiny, handsome face and hair so blond it was yellow, with the bright, sunny sheen of a cheap butter substitute. He wore a V-neck sweater draped over his shoulders. His shirt was aristocratic and striped, with a heraldic crest embroidered on the breast pocket.

"I was sent by the U.S. government to get you across the border," said the boy spy. "As I said, my name is Taylor Quizmo, Secret Agent." He pulled out his wallet and flipped it open. "License to Kill," he said, flashed a card in front of everyone, and snapped the wallet closed.

"Um, did that say 'License to Kill'?" Katie asked. "Because I thought it was a learner's permit."

"It is. A special learner's permit. License to Drive. And Kill. Well, the killing isn't specifically included on the piece of paper. You can't have that kind of thing written down. When you're in a Ugandan prison and they're really turning the thumbscrews on you, you can't have pieces of paper that say, blah blah blah, this guy can kill, he's vitally important to our national security, et cetera."

Jasper was extremely delighted to meet him. "So you are Agent Q. It must be thrilling to be a boy spy," he said, practically hopping. "I suspect you are issued some excellent gadgets. Perhaps you're even given them in underground rooms."

Taylor nodded, ducking his lips modestly. "Yes, there are a fair number of special ops gadgets attached to the position. And underground rooms. This, for example, looks like a Megaluxe

Game Wedge™, but in fact it shoots sleeping gas." He held up his game. "You saw it in action. It also plays Neutron Soccer IV. My high score is twenty-five thousand." He snapped once. "Shakin' and quakin'. What's your high score?" he asked Jasper. "Your best score?"

"I've never played Neutron Soccer IV."

Taylor looked to Drgnan. "You? Your top score?"

Drgnan was bewildered. "I do not—"

"Sure, you're a monk. You don't have fun. I forgot." Taylor gave them all a big smile. Drgnan did not return the smile. Jasper was not looking quite as delighted at meeting a boy spy.

Quizmo explained, "Some of the congressmen I know send me out on particularly delicate missions. An adult would be noticed. Suspected. But a kid? The baddies never see what hit them. Armed with my cool gear and all the lessons I learned from spy camp, I'm ready to do battle with anyone who threatens the way we live."

Jasper looked uncomfortable. He felt exactly the same way about defending the way we live, but he wasn't sure he really liked Taylor Quizmo, who'd just appeared and taken over their little gang. He wasn't really sure he *wanted* to agree with Taylor Quizmo.

They had reached the market, just as Grzo had described. There was a lively trade in dusty root vegetables and old appliances. The kids went right over to Wilt's Fishery, a shingled restaurant with an old-time diving suit standing by the door.

They went in. There was a fishy smell. A woman stood at a little podium. She was heavily made up and wore a sweater covered with white sequins. In Doverian, she said, "Hi! Welcome to Wilt's. How many in your party?"

Taylor said, "Anyone speak the spit-noises that pass for language in this stupid state?" He chuckled.

Drgnan gave the secret agent a cold look.

Then, in Doverian, he said to the woman, "We would like a table by the bay, please. Table seventeen."

The woman showed no sign that he had said anything unusual. She nodded, crossed something off with a grease pencil, took a sheaf of menus, and said, "This way."

"She says to follow," Drgnan reported. They all walked behind her.

She led them down some stairs. Diners muttered over chowder and hexagonal crackers. She took the kids into a side room. There was a tank of lobsters, and some basins of fish on ice laid out in beds of parsley.

The woman said to Drgnan, "There's someone at table seventeen right now. Please wait here. It will be ready presently."

She smiled and absently knocked out a rhythm with her ring on the lobster tank. Then she swished off to seat someone else.

"What do we do now?" said Katie.

"You just keep looking beautiful," said

Taylor Quizmo with a charming smile. "That's what you do best."

"Look!" said Lily. She pointed to the lobster tank.

One of the lobsters had trundled over to the wall of the tank and had inserted his claws into slits. He turned them back and forth, as if repeating a combination.

"Sentient lobsters!" exclaimed Jasper.

There was a click, and the lobster tank rolled to the side. Behind it was a low secret passage.

Katie said, "Wow."

Drgnan said, "Splendid."

Taylor Quizmo looked at Drgnan like the monk was an idiot. "You think *that* secret passage is cool? It's a fish tank." He patted Drgnan's arm. "But I guess your standards change once you've seen the Washington Monument slide aside to reveal a missile silo underneath. And once you've walked down secret passages formed out of flowing, molten lava into a control room on the bottom of the sea. Stick with me, friend."

"Should we go . . . ," started Lily, then stopped. She suddenly felt like she didn't want to talk in front of Taylor Quizmo. It seemed like he knew everything and thought people were stupid when they didn't.

Jasper, however, said, "Let's go, chums. Before someone walks in by accident and sees the secret passage."

The five kids ducked down and entered. Drgnan, the last to go through, pulled the secret door shut with a click.

Then the room was empty of people. The lights buzzed over the blanched fish. The tank bubbled. The lobsters went right back to playing solitaire, as if nothing had happened.

DRROK, THE GARDENER

There was only one lightbulb hanging from the ceiling of the secret corridor. Most of the passage was dark. They walked down it carefully. Jasper, in the lead, tapped his toe occasionally against the floor in front of him to check for holes or swiveling panels.

"Uh, where are we going?" Katie asked.

"The safe house, I assume," said Jasper. "The passage from Wilt's Fishery must be how the Resistance conceals the fact that many people come and go all the time."

"I don't call any house guarded by a lobster 'safe,'" said Taylor Quizmo. "Maybe a couple of Navy SEALs. Then we're talking."

"That was a pretty good joke," Katie admitted. "Lobster, then seals."

"I like a lady to laugh," said Taylor Quizmo. "It shows her teeth."

Annoyed, Katie said, "I didn't mean that I—"

"Shhh!" said Jasper.

"What's wrong, kid?" asked Taylor. "You don't like a good joke?"

Jasper didn't respond. He just waved his hand.

Then they all heard it. A grating sound, like metal scraping.

They were right under the bulb. Everything around them was dark.

A voice echoed down the corridor.

It challenged them in Doverian, a mass of spluttering syllables.

Drgnan replied in his slender, musical voice.

Another few questions. This time, the others could hear that Drgnan was introducing them all by name. *"Jasperi Dashku, knb technonautika . . . dn Lilia Gefeltaku, srt wum . . . dn*

Katia Mulliganaku . . . vlerg jyt Horror Hollow, *nyerc vm qulignamrt. Ctassm knb Taylori Quizmoku pyet, Ssfrt Kyelp. Wt kyelprt dn utr trznmn Kongreszi United Shtatii dyakrt.*"

More back-and-forth. The voice seemed to be much friendlier. Drgnan even laughed at one point.

Then there was a resounding metal clank—a screech—and a heavy, bolted door was thrown open at the end of the passage. A block of light thudded down in front of them. They walked toward it.

A guard with a machine gun was at the end, welcoming them. They each shook his hand, and he said, in a friendly, grumbly Delawarian accent, "Good hello. Good hello."

They came out in a courtyard of old yellow brick, ancient stone, and old, rotting woodwork. The house was an antique one, built in Wilmington's glory days, when all the great families of the place lived around atria, or enclosed yards. As bare as the houses were on the outside, the inside was lively with colorful ornament: monsters carved on pillars; scenes from the great Doverian epics painted on the second-floor balconies; dormers colored with bright morning shades; and all over the walls, ancient frescoes of flowers and fruits, now only ghostly, though still ripe. Girls played jump rope in the shadow of an old 1940s car that was filled with potted flowers. A baby boy ran a toy truck across the bricks, growling the sound of shifting gears, which are the same in every language. Vegetables grew in a little garden, and lush, tropical plants hung on long rope braids from the upper stories.

A man with a smart face and a clever goatee came forward, his mouth curled with pleasure, and bowed to them. He wore a dusty suit. His shirt collar was open, and he still carried a trowel in his hand. He had, apparently, been gardening.

"Greetings, children," he said. "I am Drrok, the gardener here. I shall look after you until it is time for you to leave."

They all introduced themselves—but the introductions were rushed. "Sir," said Jasper, "there is dire news to report. One of our number has been kidnapped by the Ministry of Silence and taken up to the Castle."

Drrok touched himself on the forehead and asked with horror and concern when it had happened, where, how, and other details. Drgnan answered in Doverian.

By this point, several older girls—teenagers— had come out on one of the balconies. They were staring at the boys and whispering. They especially seemed to stare at Taylor Quizmo. He looked up, saw the chicks, concealed a smile, then gave up and winked at them all. When he winked, they giggled.

"Taylor," said Jasper, "we have to think about how we're going to help Bvletch."

"Don't worry about it, kid," said Taylor. "I have to think about my public." He gave a cute little wave at his admirers.

Jasper turned away with a frown.

Drrok, the gardener, called for soldiers, and

a couple came out of one of the apartments and rushed to his side. Drgnan and Drrok clearly were explaining the situation with Bvletch to them. Lily hated to think of what might be happening to Bvletch at that very moment. She knew he would be pulled, struggling, from that hay truck and frog-marched through the Castle halls, down to its dreaded dungeons and interrogation chambers. She pictured his cheeks, spotted with blackheads, being slapped by stooges. She couldn't bear it.

Taylor had sat lightly on a planter made out of part of a pillar. His legs were crossed at the ankle and he stretched back, carefully retucking the folds of the sweater that hung around his neck. As the girls up on the balcony tittered, he took out his detonator-wristwatch and cleaned it lovingly.

Lily was trying to figure out what the soldiers of the Resistance were saying about Bvletch. She couldn't catch enough words. She had learned a few by listening for the last several days—*knb* was "boy," *kragb* was "Castle"—but that wasn't enough to go on.

"It's kind of a pain, really," Taylor announced, "attracting the kind of attention I do wherever I go. Not great for a master spy."

Lily looked around to see who he might be talking to. No one else was listening. She guessed he was talking to her. She didn't really want to talk to him. She nodded vaguely and kept her ears trained on the conversation between the members of the Resistance and Drgnan.

"There's no way I can stay incognito," said Taylor. "I mean, what *is* it with you women?"

It sounded weird to Lily, being referred to as a woman. She didn't want to be rude, but she kind of wished he would stop talking.

"I mean, sure, I'm good-looking, but come on, not *that* good-looking. Not good-looking enough to explain all this attention I get all the time." He waved back again to the girls on the balcony.

Lily saw the two soldiers talking seriously

together. One of them nodded vigorously. It looked like they were coming to some kind of decision.

"I mean," said Taylor Quizmo, "what do you think?"

Lily pretended she hadn't heard.

Taylor said, "I'm not that good-looking, really. I'm really not. What do you think? I guess you think I'm okay . . . hm?"

She glanced back at him. She nodded softly, and then said politely, "I'm sorry, I'm listening to them."

"You nodded."

She nodded again.

"You nodded that I'm okay."

Lily turned away from him.

Taylor insisted, "What do you mean, 'okay'?"

She didn't answer.

"What do you mean by that? By nodding 'okay'?"

"Don't worry."

"So you think just okay."

Lily was getting embarrassed and angry now. She didn't normally get angry, but Bvletch was in danger, and all this spoiled spy would talk about was his own face. Lily wouldn't even turn to look at him.

"How can you say that?" Taylor said. "That I'm just 'okay'?"

"I didn't say that."

"Those were your exact words. Look, I have girls from New York calling me all the time. I guess they think I'm better than 'okay.' They really know, there in New York. They know what a good-looking guy looks like. Those New York girls."

"Good," said Lily, trying to be nice. "That's good. Maybe you can get a date with one or something when we get to New Jersey."

"Oh, but you, you're too good for me," he said. "That's what you mean."

"No," said Lily. "Could we not talk about this right now?"

"Because you—Lily What's-Your-Name—you're too good for someone who once shared an ice-cream sandwich with a nineteen-year-old Russian countess."

"I don't think they have countesses anymore," said Lily. "I'm listening to the—"

"Oh, they do! They have countesses, and countesses have ice-cream Chipwiches!"

"Excuse me," said Jasper Dash. "I think—"

"What *is* it with you, kid, and the shushing? You going to librarian school or something?"

"Librarians," said Jasper hotly, "are the guardians of public knowledge."

Taylor laughed richly. "More like the guardians of the Dewey decimal system."

"By the sulphur tides of Io! I do not think you should laugh at a profession that ensures that every American citizen may—"

"*Please,* children!" said Drrok with annoyance. "We are trying to save your friend! Stop the silly *fighting!*"

At this, Lily and Jasper were overcome with

shame. They went from feeling almost like adults to feeling 100%, 120%, even 200% like children. Lily couldn't believe that because of Taylor Quizmo's weird conversation, now the Resistance thought they were squabbling, loud little brats. She wanted to sink through the cobblestones.

Jasper, she noticed, was blushing.

Drrok gave a few final comments. He bowed to the soldiers. They bowed back and ran off.

"We have spies inside the Castle," said Drrok. "They will tell us what has become of the boy."

"Spies inside the Castle?" Jasper repeated. "Swell."

Drrok nodded grimly. "It is our mission to try to infiltrate the Governing Committee's ranks and get our hands on the list of all the secret government agents in the city of Wilmington. Then we will make their names known to everyone in town, and nobody will be fooled by the Autarch's evil spies anymore."

"You'd have to get up pretty early to fool Taylor Quizmo," said Taylor Quizmo.

Drrok ignored him. He said, "Do not worry for the moment, children. We will seek out news of your friend."

After this, he showed the kids to their rooms—one for the boys, one for the girls. There were no beds, but the brick floors were warmed by flues, and he said that they would be comfortable in their sleeping bags. Lily started to get the idea that Drrok, the gardener, wasn't really the gardener. He seemed like he was in charge of the safe house. He asked the kids if there were any other questions.

Katie asked about the lobsters. Lily had wanted to, but she felt too shy to talk. She was already intimidated by Taylor Quizmo—and now she felt completely humiliated because Drrok had reminded them that they had to be quiet. But Drrok did not seem to be angry anymore. And certainly, Lily was wondering about the lobsters.

"Ah, the lobsters," said Drrok. "Indeed. They guard the door for us."

"And you *eat* them?" said Katie.

Drrok laughed. "No! No, you never eat a sentient lobster. They are as smart as you or me."

Jasper asked, "Are they part of the Resistance movement, then?"

Sorrowfully, Drrok nodded. "The Autarch is hated even by lobsters."

Taylor Quizmo whistled. "Coo-whee," he said. "When even seafood hates you . . ."

"They are not," said Drrok forcefully, "*seafood.* They are allies *disguised* as seafood."

Jasper said, "I think that's rather big of them."

Drrok nodded stiffly.

"They are poets," he said, "and painters, and they have a curious kind of silent drama that they perform in shawls. Their small black eyes are very expressive and darling."

"Darling?" said Taylor. "You mean 'yummy,' old man."

Drrok frowned.

Things weren't going very well for the kids, making friends with people from the Resistance movement.

And things weren't going very well for young Bvletch in the depths of Wilmington Castle, either.

THE GLOVES COME OFF

At first, hay, later rock, some cement—all of these complicated, rough surfaces . . . bobbing in front of Bvletch's eyes as he gradually awoke . . .

The truck was passing through huge metal gates, above which hung a sign that read KRAGB VILMINGTONIKA (Wilmington Castle), SSFRT KYELPII DOCHLA! (Secret Agents Welcome!). Bvletch shook his head. The worst thing that could happen to a friend of the Resistance had happened to him. He was being hauled into the Castle for questioning. Soon he would sit before the servants of the Autarch.

"Come on," the guards said to him, bundling him out of the back of the truck. He was sore and still dazed. He stepped gingerly on the cobblestones and stumbled. He was in a smoke-streaked courtyard. At the old windows high up, soldiers were posted. They carried big guns and peered down at him.

His whale-and-spaniel shorts were bristling with hay. It had gotten stuck in the pockets.

They led him inside.

They passed great flights of stone steps, down which the princes of Wilmington once swept with their brides and trains. Now many of the stained-glass windows had been smashed and replaced with particle board.

"The Committee is very interested in talking to you," one of the guards told Bvletch. "They have a few questions."

"They'll ask real gently," said another guard. "'Pretty please.'"

Then both guards laughed kind of meanly.

Bvletch felt awful. For days he had been feeling bad. He had been feeling alone. He was a very tenderhearted person, and so it was difficult for him to be snooty and sarcastic to Drgnan and Grzo all the time. He hated sneering and making up insults. In a strange way, he felt better being mocked by the guards.

But now he was more alone than he ever could have imagined.

The great hall, the ballroom, the audience chamber—all these had been turned into workrooms for hundreds of agents who ran New Castle County's spy network. The huge rooms had once been elegant, but now they were crammed with desks. On the walls were frescoes of court life in antique times, back when counts and damsels rode out to hunt for unicorns, and when all the great families of Wilmington would open wide the gates of their tall, faceless palaces and come out into the streets for festivals.

Now holes had been drilled in the paintings so that wires could pass through the walls. The head of a dancing prince on the wall had been smashed to make way for a pneumatic tube that rushed messages from one office to another. There were wires everywhere, hanging from brackets, clamped to the walls, nailed onto wooden posts. On the desks were old computers—big, lumpy monitors yellowed with age, and dot matrix printers chattering away while rolls of paper slowly chugged onto the floor, crammed with lists of allies and aliases and what free gifts they had requested for turning in their friends and family members.

Men and women from the Ministry of Silence looked up from their computers and watched Bvletch pass with disgust in their eyes, with reproach, with pity, with glee.

He stared at his feet so he wouldn't have to see them.

He came to a low, arched door, and the guards pushed him through it. He found himself in the jail. A man in a black linen hood and a caftan made of body odor led Bvletch along a row of cells. In each one was an enemy of the Autarch. They looked up blankly at the new prisoner, then their heads drifted back down onto the wet hay that surrounded them.

The black-hooded jailor was about to throw Bvletch into a cell when a guard behind him said, "The Committee wants to see him now."

Bvletch was startled. He thought he would have a few hours to compose himself.

"They want to see if he'll squeal about where this safe house is."

Bvletch decided, right then and there, that he was not going to let them know anything.

But now he was shoved along farther, and through another door.

It was a dark, dark chamber. There was only one shaft of light. It shone on a little wooden grade-school chair. The chair had shackles attached to the floor on either side of it. Motes of dust floated through the spotlight above it.

Bvletch was seated roughly in the chair. His hands were clamped into the shackles.

The guards stepped away, out of the circle of light.

A long time passed. Bvletch's eyes started to adjust to the brilliance and shade. He began to pick out objects ranged around the edges of the room. They were machines. Awful machines. He could not see well enough to make out their mechanisms, but their purpose was clear.

Evil, evil machines, glinting and waiting.

Bvletch decided they could never make him talk. He thought of Drgnan, Lily, Katie, and Jasper off at the safe house, counting on his silence. He thought of the single file of monks making their way through the wilderness to their new home. Though he didn't know where exactly it was now, he did know things the Autarch would be interested to find out: Bvletch knew that Vbngoom had moved. He knew that it had relocated somewhere in the western reaches of the Newark Mountains. And the Autarch must never find either of these things out, under any circumstances. Bvletch closed his eyes and tried not to cry.

"Rise for the entrance of the Governing Committee of Wilmington!" barked a guard.

Bvletch rose as best he could, being partially held down with chains.

A door in the far wall slammed open. He could hear it but not see it.

Then the Governing Committee entered.

Footsteps approached. Only one set of footsteps.

The Committee was a tallish, thinnish man in a long, black coat. The coat had a row of tiny buttons all the way from his neck to his knees. The Committee wore a high collar, and his hands were clasped in front of him. His face was long, like the sole of a shoe.

"I am the Committee," he said. "Sit."

Bvletch sat.

The young monk waited for the rest of the members of the Committee to enter.

But the man who had just sat down opposite him, barely visible outside the ring of brilliant light, said, "We aren't waiting for anyone.

I am the whole Committee. After some disagreements a few years ago, a few of my fellow members unfortunately had to resign. And fall into the ocean. A shame. I was sorry to lose them. The work? It is a hard burden for me to bear alone, but I manage." The Governing Committee sighed. He looked around. His face looked like white, powdered leather. "So. To begin. You know the old saying? 'We have ways of making you talk'? It is true, citizen." His voice was slow and soft and scratchy.

"I wish," the Committee explained, "to hear about your home. Who does not enjoy a memory of home when he is far from it? Our questions shall begin there, child." He waited. There was silence in the chamber. "It is no use resisting," the Governing Committee hissed. "I rule here with an iron fist." He held up his white hand and curled the fingers cruelly.

He looked at it. He frowned unhappily.

He called a guard's name. The guard stepped forward.

The Committee said, "Shouldn't I have some metal gloves? I feel like this kind of thing should be done with metal gloves on."

The guard cleared his throat. "We got you some metal gloves, Committee, sir. We had them made up."

"No. No, you did not. Those were not gloves, citizen. Those were *mittens.* There is a difference. A key difference, soldier. Metal mittens do not frighten people."

"Why weren't they gloves, sir?"

"Because gloves have individual fingers. And mittens just have a kind of a big . . . finger blob, I suppose you could say. With a separate thumb."

"There's not much of a difference, Committee, sir."

"That's a huge difference," the inquisitor snapped.

"You don't need your fingers for interrogating, sir."

The Committee pressed his palms to his

eyes, then folded his hands in front of him. "Citizen," said the Committee with a sigh, "that is not the point."

"Well," said the guard, "so what *is* the p—?"

"Go ask the ocean," spat the Committee, and pressed a button.

The guard disappeared into a trapdoor that presumably led to the sea. There was a long, echoing yelp.

The Committee turned back to Bvletch. "Fine. Good, citizen, he said. "Shall we begin?" He stood, drawing himself up to his full witch-broom length. He pondered for a moment, looking shrewdly at his monkish prisoner.

"It really would be better if I had metal gloves, wouldn't it?" he asked.

In the courtyard of the safe house, it was a beautiful evening. The air was warm and luscious. The courtyard smelled green and full of the fragrance of fruit. There were candles lit in alcoves, and a little band played the old folk songs of Delaware while a few dreamy girls sang along, braiding one another's hair.

Katie sat beside Drgnan on a flight of steps.

"They're really nice to help us," said Katie.

"The monks of Vbngoom and the Resistance have always helped one another," said Drgnan. "We all wish with our whole hearts that the elected Governor of Delaware would be restored to the throne and would rule with benignity and peace as in the days of yore."

"When exactly was yore?"

Drgnan and she smiled at each other—but their smiles did not last long. They were both worried.

"We all must help one another," said Drgnan. "The legs of the donkey do not quarrel. They do not go off in different directions in huffs."

Katie squeezed her hands between her knees. "I'm worried about Bvletch," she said. "What do you think is happening to him right now?"

Drgnan did not even want to answer. He envisioned the interrogation rooms that must be up at the Castle: awful machines; evil, evil machines, glinting and waiting.

He could not bear to think of his spiritual brother locked up there.

Katie whispered, "I wish I were at home." Then she looked quickly at Drgnan and said, "I mean—not without Bvletch. But all of us. I wish we were already there. I can't stand all these people having to hide, and worrying about who's going to turn them in, and . . ." Katie felt like she was about to cry at the thought of all of it—the Castle looming above the sooty city, the burned-out hills of Brandywine, the hopelessness of it all. "I wish I were home and my father was with me," she admitted. She pictured her dad, his hair as dark as his suit. She didn't feel strong, suddenly, like a girl used to fighting mutant armies with a toilet plunger. She wanted to hear her father say, "Hey, honey. I'm right here. Don't be afraid."

But Katie's father didn't even know where she was. He and Katie's mom were probably panicking, calling the police, terrified.

And Drgnan Pghlik thought of his fellow monks wandering through the wilderness. Their safety rested with him and with Bvletch. He thought of his home, the monastery, standing empty, waiting to be filled again with novices playing volleyball. He thought of the hundreds of miles between him and his new home. He thought of Bvletch, somewhere in the dark, surrounded by cranks and cogs. Buried in a dungeon so deep that no one could hear his cries for help.

"We'll get there," said Katie, "won't we? We'll get back to Pelt and you'll see it? And my house? I'll show you around?"

Drgnan could only nod. He could not speak.

"And Bvletch will be there, won't he?" said Katie.

Drgnan looked at her, and then he looked away.

They both were so scared, so worried, that they hardly noticed when their hands slid together. They didn't even look down when their hands met and held fast to each other, as if to say, *It will be okay.* Then Katie realized what was happening, and she felt a flood of joy—and a withering blast of guilt at feeling a flood of joy—and then the joy again, too strong to be frozen out—and Drgnan looked at her wonderingly.*

Meanwhile, across the courtyard, at a picnic table, Lily couldn't get rid of Taylor Quizmo, Secret Agent. It had taken her all afternoon, but she had finally realized what was going on: Taylor was not going to go away until she said he was cute. But there was no way she was going to tell him he was cute, because Lily always tried to tell the truth, and she thought he was kind of ugly and mean.

At first Jasper sat with them at the table. A waiter asked them if he could bring them anything from the restaurant. They all said they wanted hamburgers, which sounded great, until Taylor started saying spoiled-kid things to the waiter like, "We don't want just any old cow-

---

*I hate to interrupt this very romantic moment, but I thought I would mention that outside, in the streets around the safe house, several black vans and cars were pulling up alongside the blank stone walls. Vegetable sellers were looking carefully up and down the street. Some of the vegetable sellers twitched their mustaches, as if their mustaches were not their own. There was a dim murmur of walkie-talkie crackle.

butt, friend." He chuckled richly. "You know what would be superb? Some bleu cheese on top, some fresh minced chives—fresh, mind you, otherwise they just taste like old onion—a dab of Worcestershire sauce . . . What?"

The waiter said, "We don't have bleu cheese, kid."

"I forgot," said Taylor, winking at his two dinner companions. "We're not in Kansas anymore. All right, friend, what say to mixing some crumbled feta in with the ground sirloin, a little ground pork sausage, virgin olive oil, some fresh basil and dill, a red onion minced really fine—uncooked before you put it in the meat—all whipped up into patties and then topped with juicy slices of a thick heirloom tomato?"

"We're kind of a fried-clam joint."

"I'm fine with just a normal burger," said Lily quickly. She could see that the waiter was getting irritated.

"Ditto for me," said Jasper.

"I like the finer things in life," said Taylor,

casting an arch glance at Lily. "Have you heard of the Serbian cevapcici? Ringing the changes on the old burger of yesteryear. Some lamb, some paprika—"

"Three burgers," exclaimed the waiter, scribbling on his pad. "Want Kraft slices on top?"

"Yes, please!" said Lily.

The man nodded and walked off.

Taylor said, "I've been around the world in my line of work, being a secret agent, you know, which is what I *do*. And I guess I've come to appreciate a good hotel and a fine meal. Not that we're going to get either one here." He chuckled. "Cheers," he said, "to us." He lifted up his Coca-Cola to click it against their Coca-Colas. "Normally I prefer to drink an Italian cremosa. A dash of amaretto soda syrup, seltzer, some cream . . . or something like a Vietnamese ginger cordial. Also excellent." He looked intensely at Lily. "Which do you prefer? But I forget. You're a Coke woman yourself. Aren't you? Diet, I hope." He looked at her face and her shapeless T-shirt. "Yes, ma'am."

This was incredibly mean, but Lily didn't even care. She and Jasper felt tired and awkward. They were both worried about Bvletch. They hadn't heard a word from the Resistance's spies in the Castle. They'd spent a difficult afternoon waiting. They'd hung around the courtyard. A television was blaring, but there was nothing on. There were just programs like *The Adorable Autarch's Hit Parade* or spy game shows in which the Autarch's spies publicly unmasked other spies—game shows with names like *I've Blown Your Cover!* and *This Is Your Double Life!*

The five kids had watched some of *This Is Your Double Life!* with Drgnan translating. A spy was called up onstage from out of the studio audience, and then a bunch of informants he'd known in the past denounced him and exposed him while he tried to guess who they were. (A female voice: "We had a beautiful dinner together in Vienna. You named a new species of poisonous tropical flower after me."—While the spy in the spotlight guessed, "Is it—is it Ldmilla? Ldmilla Brblik? . . . No. . . . No, it can't be. . . . You've betrayed me! Ldmilla! How—how could you?!? We exchanged numbers. . . . We exchanged gunshots! But I never thought you'd turn me in. . . ." etc., etc.)

Daytime television in Wilmington was really awful.

And then they were stuck with the obnoxious Taylor Quizmo while they waited for their burgers.

Taylor took a long, steady sip of his Coke. He gave a warm smile to the other two kids. He said to Jasper, "That is so great you have your own series of books too."

"Thank you," said Jasper.

"I think I remember them. They were published a long, long time ago, right? With all kinds of cute, old-timey inventions in them?"

Taylor took another long draft of his Coke. "I mean, I have a series about me and my adventures as a boy spy, but I don't know if they're any good. I haven't read any of them myself. I just don't have time. I'm always off on another adventure! That must be one of the great things about having a series that hasn't sold any copies for fifty years—you really have time to relax. No one clamoring for you to go anywhere or do anything. That's just great."

It was apparently not just great for Jasper. The Boy Technonaut stood up. "I'm sorry," he said weakly. "I . . . I have to . . . I just remembered that I'm eating over there." He pointed rather unconvincingly at an empty corner near a little ficus tree. "Near that little tree."

He gave a weird, embarrassed bow and walked away.

If he'd really been in his usual frame of mind, he would have found an excuse to pull Lily away too. He knew, however, that wherever

Lily went, Taylor would go. And Jasper was really starting to feel that Taylor, despite his good intentions, was really not a very nice or thoughtful person.

So Lily was stuck alone at the table with Taylor. She wanted really badly to be someplace else.*

"It's . . . it's really nice of you to come and help us," said Lily. She was trying to be friendly. "If it hadn't been for you, Jasper and Drgnan would have been captured by those men in the hay. Not just Bvletch."

"Don't worry!" said Taylor. "It's all in the line of duty, as the saying goes. If any of my friends in Congress wants me to do a thing, that's all I have to know. I'm there."

"Great," said Lily. "I mean, nice. For us."

There was nothing to talk about. Lily looked

----

*I think Lily would really, *really* have wanted to be someplace else if she had known that out in the alleys around the safe house, doors to black vans were opening, and men in black sweaters, balaclavas, and bulletproof long johns were crawling out. They each had on an armband with the symbol of the Ministry of Silence: a finger across lips, as if to say, "Shhh!"

at the grain of the wood in the table. The folk songs drifted over to them.

"Do you think Bvletch is okay?" Lily asked.

"Okay? *Okay?*" Taylor rubbed Lily's arm. "Well, that's a good thought. From a good little girl." He nodded solemnly. "But there's no way he's okay. They've probably shipped him off to Fort Delaware, if they haven't already fed him to the sand sharks."

Lily stared at Taylor. "Really?" she said.

"It's the Ministry of Silence," said Taylor. "You know how they are."

"I thought sand sharks didn't eat people. That's what they say in Pelt. We have sand sharks in Smoggascoggin Bay."

"Pelt? Pelt!??" Taylor chuckled. "We aren't in Pelt anymore." He took a draw on his Coke. He smiled a pert little smile. "So," he said, "do you have any hobbies? I have a few."

Lily did not want to talk about hobbies. Who knew what was happening to Bvletch? She looked wildly around the courtyard, hoping for some excuse to get up,* anything that might distract her from the—

And she saw Katie and Drgnan holding hands. There they sat, with Katie beaming—not smiling much, but beaming, as if a secret panel in her head had opened up and a light came out on a stalk and illuminated everything in a rosy glow. Katie and Drgnan didn't move. They just sat there listening to the music, holding hands.

Lily wanted a trapdoor to open up under her and drop her into the ocean or something.

As long as sand sharks didn't eat people.

She knew it was good for Katie and for Drgnan—she was happy for them, she told herself, really happy, but—

Taylor was saying, "And I do archery." He appeared to still be talking about his hobbies without noticing she hadn't responded.

---

* If only she had known, her excuse could have been that commandos from the Ministry of Silence were crawling up the stone walls of the house on grappling hooks. That usually is a pretty good excuse to get up from the table.

"I'm no dab hand with a bow and arrow, but I guess I'm, ha, I'm good enough to pin down a Mongolian assassin at one hundred yards. And I scuba dive. And skydive. And wrestle. And wrestle while I skydive. And I play golf. Do you play golf?"

"I have," Lily admitted. She couldn't even think.

Taylor asked her, "You have? What's your handicap? In golf?"

"I always hit the little windmill."

Taylor laughed. "No, your *numerical* handicap. For example, mine's nine. Which I guess is okay. It's pretty okay." He smiled humbly. "That's what you'd call it, right? *Okay?* Since you think a lot of things are just *okay?* I guess a little nine on the golf handicap is *okay*, even by your standards? Is that right?"

The instruments played and Taylor kept on talking and Lily's head was ringing, ringing, ringing.

Or was that Taylor's cell phone?

He took it out and looked at the screen. "It's Washington!" he said. He anxiously jabbed at the buttons. "They must want to coordinate our escape!" He hit the send button three times in a row by accident, and the phone shot poison darts into the bushes. By that time he had answered it. He put his hand over his ear, shooting dirty glances at the musicians. "I can't . . . One second . . ." He held up a finger and winked at Lily. He said to her, "Will you permit me?"

She shrugged.

"I mean, will you step away from the table so I can talk?"

She got up gladly. She took her plate and napkin and started walking over toward Jasper.

"*And,*" Taylor called after her, "could you tell those musicians to shut up? I'm trying to talk to a senator, here."

She did no such thing.

When Taylor was done, he came over to Lily and Jasper's corner. The two friends were sitting with their knees almost touching. They had gotten their hamburgers and were eating them silently.

"All done," said Taylor.

Lily looked up at him.

"You all right?" he asked.

"I hope you had a good phone call," said Lily miserably.

"Depends on what you mean by 'good.' Because I had to tell him that you guys had lost one of your friends to the Ministry of Silence when I ran into you. He said the plan may change for getting you out of the state tomorrow. Who knows? They'll call back. What a day."

"Could we use your cell phone?" Lily asked. "We'd like to call our parents. Katie's and my cell phones don't have a signal in Delaware, and we don't have enough coal to power Jasper's."

"Sorry," said Taylor, giving her a friendly smile. "I would, but it's government property. Can't let anyone else touch it. And you probably wouldn't like it, anyway. It's probably just *okay* to you. I wouldn't want you to use just an *okay* cell phone."

With that, he walked away.

And everyone was relieved.

At this point, there could have been a conversation between Lily and Jasper. Maybe Lily would have even told her friend nervously that she kind of liked Drgnan Pghlik. Or maybe Jasper would have guessed it without her telling him. It would have been hard for Lily to tell Jasper, especially because Lily wanted Katie to be happy, and in some ways, she was glad that Katie and Drgnan were holding hands.

It also would have been hard for Lily to tell Jasper about liking Drgnan because of the commandos who were crawling across the slate roof of the old mansion, eager to drop down and capture everyone in the courtyard.

Lily and Jasper sat silently. Neither of them looked over toward Drgnan and Katie. They watched the musicians play the folk tunes of

Delaware, and the girls sing while one rocked the baby's cradle with her foot. They watched Taylor Quizmo eat his hamburger.

Lily suddenly felt a rush of longing for her home and her parents. She just wanted to be around normal things, like her bookshelves and her desk and a comfy chair that didn't turn out to be Mrglik, Delaware's finest furniture-imitating spy. She didn't want to have to watch carefully all the time and always be on her guard. She wanted to listen to her mom and dad talk over the news of the day, sitting at their kitchen table—without any mention of tyrants or dictators or obnoxious spies or anything crazy and dangerous. Just one more day, she told herself, and she'd be back in her living room, eating a bowl of ice cream. Just one more day.

A guard rushed into the courtyard, wearing a muddy *blrga* shirt and, tied around his head, a necktie.

"I wonder if something is wrong," mused

Jasper. "That fellow looks mightily churned up."

The guard went over to Drrok, the gardener, and whispered something to him. Drrok smiled and nodded and spoke to the musicians. They began another tune.

Lily shrugged. "I guess it was a request," she said.

"They take requests?" said Jasper. He sighed. "I wonder if they'd do the theme from *It Came from Outer Space.* It always reminds me of home."

The musicians' lazy tune floated over the courtyard, but nothing in the courtyard itself was lazy, suddenly. The girls had risen up and taken the baby, and they were filing out as quickly as possible. They blew out candles as they went. Men and women who'd been sitting up on the balconies disappeared. Lily and Jasper looked around in consternation.

If only they'd known, everyone was leaving because of the music. Not that it was bad music. But the words to the music, in Doverian, went:

You tell me

you love me.

You tell me

you care.

The guard tells me

we are surrounded

by commandos.

The commandos of my heart.

And also ones with super crossbows.

I mean, the real kind of commandos.

Get up and leave, my sweet one.

Quickly, silently.

Get up and leave, my dear one.

Because this place we love

is ours no more.

No more, my dear.

So run.

The men crawling across the roof heard the
song dimly, muffled, below, and thought that

it was just a love song. They thought everyone was still gathered in the atrium, motionless, looking at the candles and the stars. They did not see people scampering to grab their most important possessions—shoe boxes of letters or bags of photos or an old corduroy rabbit on a bed. They did not see people rushing down flights of stairs—in bare feet, so as not to create a ruckus—and unclamping secret doors into the sewers.

Drgnan, dragging Katie by the wrist, rushed to Lily and Jasper's side. He whispered quickly, "Come on! We've got to run! The Ministry of Silence found us! They're invading!"

Lily and Jasper asked no questions. They stood up and prepared to follow Drgnan. Drgnan, meanwhile, looked toward Drrok for guidance. Drrok gestured with his head toward the secret door into the restaurant.

Jasper started to wave at Taylor Quizmo.

Taylor kept eating fries.

For a few seconds longer.

Before the men in black dangled like evil worms from the rooftops, masks over their faces, ropes in their hands, handcuffs on their belts, and malice everywhere.

Dangling they came, their teeth grit, and they slid toward the earth. They did not speak as they landed. Their soft-soled espionage boots touched, finally, the cobblestones, and then they looked around to see who they could grab.

The musicians lay down their instruments without a word. In their hands they had dart guns. They began to fire on the assailants.

Jasper, Lily, Drgnan, Katie, and Taylor were hidden in the shadows behind some tropical tree in a vat. They couldn't make it to the secret door they had originally come through. They would have to sneak along the wall.

"We arrest you," called one of the commandos to Drrok, "in the name of the Governing

Committee of Wilmington and His Terrifying Majesty, the Awful and Adorable Autarch of Dagsboro!"

He winced as a dart hit his neck—then his eyes crossed, and he collapsed into slumber.

At that, all the commandos pulled out their handheld crossbows and began firing. The musicians blocked shots with their dulcimers and slapped bolts out of the air with their goo-tars. But there were too many commandos and not enough musical instruments. If it had been a whole symphony orchestra, maybe they would have stood a chance. But as it was, they were just a quartet, and more soldiers were sliding down the ropes.

Lily watched the events in horror. "They're going to get Drrok!" she said.

Indeed, the soldiers had hit Drrok in the leg with a drugged crossbow bolt. He held up his dart gun, but his hand was unsteady. He was getting woozy. He shot one guard with a dart—and carefully collapsed in a head-butt, knocking out another—but then didn't rise, himself.

The commandos clustered in to pick him up.

And Lily realized—the Ministry of Silence had probably found this safe house because of her and her friends. Either spies had followed them here, or—oh no—she didn't even want to think about this—or they had forced the information out of Bvletch.

Bvletch!

Miserably she watched Drrok, the leader of this cell of the Resistance, get lifted up from the ground, sleeping. She watched the soldiers handcuff him.

And then she watched one notice her—and shoot a crossbow bolt right at her pale face in the shadows.

THE GIRLS IN FLAMES

THWACK!

The crossbow bolt buried itself deep.

In the trunk of the shrub, which Jasper had yanked over to the side just in time.

"They've seen us, fellows!" he cried. "We must prepare for a furious fight!"

"We've got to get out of here!" said Katie.

"Through the secret passage," said Lily, pointing to the door about twenty feet away.

Commandos were running over toward them.

And Drgnan was climbing the shrubby tree.

"Drgnan!" hissed Jasper. "What's the dodge?"

"Diversion, brother," said Drgnan—and Jasper seemed immediately to know what he meant.

Drgnan reached his hand down toward Katie. "Take my hand," he said.

She did so. In a glow.

"Pull," said Drgnan, and she pulled, and the tree bent back with him clutching it between his knees. Katie's muscles bulged. Then Drgnan yelled, "LET GO!" and Katie spread her fingers—

And Drgnan went flying through the air, as if from a vaultapult.

He hurtled—a plaid stripe—overhead—and the soldiers fired, craning their necks as he lofted over them—

While the kids, behind the whickering shrub, ran for the secret passage.

Drgnan hit the far wall of the courtyard. He would have fallen and broken his neck if he hadn't grabbed one of the black ropes hanging from the grappling hooks—which allowed him to kick the wall and swing back out.

He arced out over the mob of soldiers, trounced one who was still sliding down a nearby rope, and then spun toward the secret door.

His friends were already through.

"Down with the Autarch!" he called defiantly. "Long live the Governor of Delaware!"

The crossbow bolts were flying around him in swarms. He let go of the rope—rolled through the air—and hopped into the hole where Jasper held the door to the secret passage open.

Drgnan landed running, puffing, and Jasper stood for one glorious moment, facing the commandos, smiling at them jauntily. Then—just as a barrage of crossbow bolts were about to hit him—he slammed the door shut. He heard thunks like freezing rain on a tin roof.

But he was already jogging after his friends down the secret corridor into Wilt's Fishery.

Lily didn't want to be rude, but Taylor Quizmo, Secret Agent, was still eating his fries one by one as they ran. "Um," she said, "um,

Taylor? Don't you have a cell phone that shoots darts? Which you could use?"

"When I'm done with my french fries," he said, "I'll mop up these jokers in no time flat."

"Okay," said Lily, "but could you at least not dip each fry in the ketchup first?"

"*Fine*, Lily," said Taylor, throwing his arms wide so the container of fries and the paper cup of ketchup flew and splattered all over the secret passage. "I won't even *finish* my fries. Are you happy now? Are you '*okay*'?"

"Well, you know, Drrok got taken prisoner, and the others have lost their home, and it's kind of our fault, so I wonder whether—"

"You are just *impossible*," said Taylor. "I can't believe I am even hanging out with you."

Katie was rolling the secret door in the restaurant out of the way.

Meanwhile, at the other end of the corridor, the commandos had charged in, crossbows stinging like wasps.

The kids tumbled out into the fish larder at

the restaurant. They slid the lobster tank/secret door closed and ran for the exit.

The restaurant was not only deserted—with tables overturned and fried clams all over the floor—but it was on fire. The windows were all smashed, as if the commandos had kicked their way in, and candles had been knocked over and now the tablecloths were burning with a thick, greasy smell. Flames were rising all over the dining room. Coughing and whacking the smoke away from them, the five stumbled past the bathrooms.

Just as the kids were about to run out the front door of the joint—just as they were almost home free—Katie stopped in her tracks, looking horrified.

"THE SENTIENT LOBSTERS!" she exclaimed.

Dear reader. Dear, dear reader. Here we find ourselves, you and me, engaged in a book in which someone has just exclaimed, in all seriousness, "The sentient lobsters!"

195

How did we end up here? Did we make some mistake along the way? Aren't there books on geology, or the ancient Greek theater, or the art of Japanese flower arranging, to study?

I ask you, *Isn't there something else we should be reading?*

And I tell you: *No*.

Because you and me, we understand that important things don't always seem important. We understand that looks can be deceptive. We understand that Katie's question was in fact a very important one. Why? Because it's important to think about the fact that the Ministry of Silence might seize upon the tank of sentient lobsters who guard the safe house for the Resistance—and it's important to consider that if Katie didn't yell "THE SENTIENT LOBSTERS!" the lobsters might have found themselves abandoned and forgotten, sad eyed and with drooping claws—while the restaurant burned—and their briny water heated up—and the littlest lobsters wept for help—as the flames rose. . . .

AND THAT CANNOT HAPPEN, MY FRIENDS!

"She's right!" said Lily. "Those lobsters are trapped in their tank! We've got to save them!"

"Save them?" said Taylor. "Forget it! They're boiled! They're bisque! They're Newburg! They're lobster thermidor!"

"They are poets!" said Katie. "They're painters! They're playwrights! They're singers!"

"They're not singers," said Drgnan.

"You know what I mean," said Katie.

Lily and Katie ran back into the fish larder.

The commandos were just starting to push the lobster tank out of the way, so that they could crawl out from the little door behind it—when Lily, panicking, threw a dead fish at the lead soldier's head! He ducked, slipped, and fell backward.

Katie, meanwhile, was wheeling the tank away from the wall, saying, "Don't worry! We've got you!"

Unfortunately, moving the tank exposed the secret passage entirely—and now the commandos struggled out into the larder as Katie and Lily scarpered.

The two girls rolled the tank between them, giving it a shove and pulling up their feet so they rode it, soaring, into the dining room.

The flames in the restaurant were billowing. Lily and Katie looked about in terror. They weren't sure they could make it back to the front door, where they saw Jasper, Taylor, and Drgnan waving their hands and calling. The fire was between them and the exit.

But the commandos were close behind them.

So the two girls did what they could.

"Under water!" Lily yelled over the crackling, and she took a deep breath—shoved off with her foot—and plunged her whole upper body into the tank. Now the tank was shooting toward the flames—so Katie, too, dunked—and the tank went hurtling through the fire—

Leaving the commandos behind.

Katie and Lily watched the flames flicker by quaintly through the green glass. Then they were on the other side, near the front door. Home free.

The boys pulled the tank out into the market square. The girls, sopping, pulled handfuls of sentient lobsters out of the water with them. "We've got to take them!" said Katie.

Lily lowered her arms into the brine. The little claws nipped at her to hold on, and she, grimacing with the pain, pulled them out. They hung from her arms, grateful for the ride. Jasper plucked some. Drgnan set two on his shoulders, where they waved their antennae about in delighted thanks and relief.

The kids left the empty tank behind them and scrambled over the cobbles.

Taylor said, "Okay, kiddies. My Hummer is parked near where I met you. If we can just get there, we'll be fine. It has, shall we say, a few extra features. A few unusual conveniences. Some things that might come in *very* useful."

Behind them, they saw troops running across the market. No one else was out in the dark lanes.

Horrified, they glimpsed, a long way down a side street, the soldiers leading along several girls in braids and *blrga* shirts. The musicians and Drrok were all handcuffed and were being hustled into the back of the Ministry's vans.

Lily's heart sank. Here there had been a safe house, a place for those who fought for democracy and freedom—a place where people had played music and been happy—hidden for years—inviting even the lobsters in—and now it was ruined.

Flames were billowing out of Wilt's Fishery.

Four commandos spotted them—ran toward them and raised their crossbows.

Lily, instinctively, ducked.

Taylor pulled out his Game Wedge™. He aimed it at the soldiers and released another cloud of sleeping gas. The commandos stumbled and crumpled.

Jasper frowned. He looked at the sleeping stooges. He had an awful feeling that Taylor Quizmo might actually be a better version of him—superior gadgets, more confidence, more knowledge of the world. He had to admit, "Good work."

"*De nada,*" said Taylor, and motioned with his hand.

The kids scrambled along a cobbled road. Now they were in the alley where Bvletch had been seized.

They turned a corner into the main thoroughfare.

Not too far up, beside a public lantern, was Taylor's red Humvee. "My mom and dad got it for me," he boasted, opening the doors so the others could clamber in. "After I stopped a little assassination attempt in the Low Countries. Just a little matter of a prime minister." He winked, though no one was looking at him. He slammed his door shut and pulled on his seat belt.

"They're coming!" said Jasper, pointing out the back window. Commandos were running out into the avenue. "Go, go, go!"

Taylor just stayed put.

"Go, brother!" said Drgnan. "The wolves approach!"

Taylor looked a little vexed. "Are . . . ," he said, "are any of you over eighteen?"

There was a frazzled silence.

"Of course none of us are over eighteen," said Katie. "What do you think?"

Taylor shifted uncomfortably. "I only have my learner's permit. It was issued specially. I'm too young to have a learner's permit usually, but for spy missions, they thought—"

"Heavens to Betsy—what are you getting at?" Jasper exclaimed.

Taylor admitted, "I can't drive. Legally. Except if I'm accompanied by an adult over eighteen years of age."

Katie thumped her head, exasperated, in her hands.

"Great Scott," swore Jasper.

Taylor seemed a little embarrassed by this.

Actually, it wasn't a bad thing. If they'd torn off up the road, there's no question that the commandos would have seen them and followed them. As it was, the commandos just ran around them, up and down alleys, trying to figure out where the kids had disappeared to.

The kids just sat tight, ducking below the windows.

Watching the soldiers run past without noticing them clearly made Taylor feel a little better. He stopped pressing his lips together so hard and instead started stroking the padded dashboard. "Yep," he said, "she's a pretty great vehicle. She can climb right over a twenty-two-inch vertical wall and drive up a sixty percent grade. I guess that's pretty good, huh? Huh? Is that *okay* enough for you? 'Cause I think it's pretty okay, and she can also traverse a forty-percent-grade side slope with a full payload of three thousand pounds, and she's equipped with an emergency parachute, and an oil slick, and bear repellent, and I don't mind saying that she can plow through up to thirty inches of—"

"Um, Taylor?" said Lily, who didn't want to be rude. "Maybe we should all keep quiet and scrunch farther down."

The sound of jackboots on cobbles shook the Hummer.

"Yeah," said Taylor, a little cowed. "We should scrunch down." He unbuckled himself. He squatted. "There's plenty of foot space to hide in," he said, somewhat glumly. "Huh? Not too shabby. Plenty of, um, legroom. For hiding."

Lily, trying to be nice, agreed, "Very . . . big and . . . spacious."

And so they all crouched in the ample legroom. They waited for the soldiers to give them up for lost.

PLUMBING THE DEPTHS IN THE
DEPTHS OF THE PLUMBING

Hours later they were safe in the sewers. The lobsters took them there.

Drrok had, over the years, created a number of plans in case the Autarch's forces should ever discover the Resistance's secret hideout. There was a hidden place deep in the sewers of Wilmington where they could all assemble and decide the next step to take.

The lobsters, of course, knew where it was, and so once the coast was clear, they led the kids through the streets and gutters. The lead lobster—his name was a movement of antennae—sat on Lily's shoulder, pointing the way with his mammoth old claws. He was a blue lobster, and his carapace was the color of a beautiful deep midnight frost.

Wilmington did not look welcoming that night. Metal shutters were pulled down over the fronts of businesses and locked. The tall windows in upper stories of buildings were dark. Shades were drawn, except when some old lady was peering out.

No one was on the streets. Once in a while, an idle man would be sitting on a street corner, whistling. When the kids passed, his tune would change.

Or a public mailbox they passed would rustle, as if someone were shifting their weight on top of letters.

Or a tree's branches would swing like a periscope to follow them.

Finally the Blue Lobster directed them down a flight of steps, through a brick archway, and into the city's sewers.

If you have read many adventure novels, you'll know that spies spend about half of their time in the sewers. They run along sewer tunnels, shooting. They find secret hideaways in sewers. They take weird funeral barges through sewers, poled along by old men in hoods. In fact, if a spy's kid wants to get a message to their mom or dad, the easiest way to do it is just to flush it down the toilet. Scribble, scribble: *Mom, don't forget I have soccer practice at three. Love, Patrick.* *FLUSH.* Two hours later, there's Mom with the minivan, out of breath and brushing poos off her lapels.

When spies aren't in sewer tunnels, they're usually crawling through air ducts. I'm not sure exactly why this is. It makes you kind of wonder: Are spies just frustrated maintenance men? Is that what spies really want to be doing? Plumbing? Air conditioner repair? I fear the day that they follow their dream, lay down their laser-gun cigarette lighters, and pick up wrenches. Our country will be in great peril, though with fewer toilets backing up and more of our houses at a uniform sixty-eight degrees Fahrenheit.

So the kids were led through passages beneath the brooding city. There, deep in the sewer tunnels, in an old, octagonal chamber with empty niches in the brick walls, the remnants of the safe house sat sadly and waited for news.

They were surprised to see the kids and the lobsters arrive. Blue Lobster waved his antennae. A guard who spoke lobster got up, held his arms straight up like antennae, and spasmed them over his head. Blue Lobster twitched back. The guard translated the story of the lobsters' escape to the other Delawarians. There was a sigh of great relief.

Otherwise, the Delawarian Resistance did not seem entirely happy to see the kids. It took a moment to understand why, but then Jasper and Lily looked at each other unhappily, and they both realized: The Delawarians believed that somehow, the kids had led the Ministry of Silence to the secret safe house and made it forever unsafe.

"Did we?" Jasper asked anxiously.

"Maybe Bvletch told the Ministry of Silence," said Lily.

"Brother Bvletch would never break under pressure," said Drgnan. "He is a monk of Vbngoom."

"But because he is a monk of Vbngoom," said a guard, "he cannot tell lies. If they have captured him and he speaks, then they know the truth about where you were headed, and about the safe house—"

"And they know that Vbngoom is no longer on the Four Peaks, but is off in the mountains to the west!" said Jasper.

Firmly, Drgnan insisted, "I do not believe we need to worry about Brother Bvletch."

"Then maybe we were followed," said Lily. "We were pretty careful, but maybe . . ." She looked around. The eyes of the refugees were accusing. Gentle, but accusing.

The refugees had lost everything. They had lost their home.

Lily asked, "Is there anyone else who might have known where the safe house was?"

The guard shook his head. "There are several safe houses and bases of operation in Wilmington, but few people know all—"

"Ah! Thanks be to the pillars of heaven that you are safe!" said a voice, echoing through the vault.

In the candlelight, the kids couldn't see who it was at first. Then Lily saw it was Grzo's friend, the van's other driver, dressed in his plainclothes disguise. He had just arrived in the octagonal chamber. He shut the metal door behind him and waved.

"It's that monk," said Katie. "The van's other driver. Grzo's friend."

"Grzo's friend?" said Drgnan. "No, he is not Grzo's friend. He just joined the monastery a day or two before we set out from . . ."

The kids all looked at one another.

"But—," said Jasper.

"I thought you knew!" said Drgnan. "I

wondered earlier about him, but I said nothing. One who does not turn on the stove never gets burned."

"Children," said the monk, whose name they didn't even know, "it is so good to see no harm befell you. Brother Grzo has been most anxious about you." He shook their hands one by one.

"Where is he, Brother?" Drgnan asked.

"He is with the van. There is a plan. A van plan. First, tell me of what has happened. I went to the safe house and found it besieged. If I had not met Byimpt here," (he indicated a guard), "I would never have known where to find you."

"Is Brother Grzo safe?"

"Far safer than you have been, I fear, brave tykes. We have been in a garage owned by the Resistance, having the van fixed and a new license plate and registration made up. Tomorrow morning—only a few hours from now—we shall board the ferry and cross to New Jersey."

"So why isn't Grzo here, sir?" Jasper challenged.

"He must stay with the van. He will meet us on the ferry. The Ministry of Silence knows to look for us and our van, so it is better that we go through the checkpoint onto the ferry in separate groups. Do not fear, children. All is arranged for our safety."

"Well, it wasn't arranged so well," said Katie. "Because Bvletch is trapped in the Castle and somehow somebody told the Ministry of Silence about the location of the safe house, so there was a raid, and now none of these people has a home. And let me repeat about Bvletch. And it's making us kind of suspicious."

"This," said the monk sadly, shaking his head, "is why it is awful to live in a land ruled by a tyrant. No one trusts his own brother or his own sister. Is that not terrible? Even the lobster weeps."

The kids did not say anything in response to this. Lily felt a nasty creeping sensation up and down her spine. She had driven with this man for hundreds of miles.

Finally Brother Drgnan broke the silence. He said, "This is the secret agent the United States government sent to help us. His name is Taylor Quizmo."

"Ah!" said the monk. "You are sent from Washington?"

"Yes. Occasionally one of my friends from the United States Senate or the House of Representatives will call me and ask me, as just a special kind of favor, to do a little job for them. Little odds and ends like stopping assassination attempts, saving the World Bank, and blowing up illegal missile silos in the jungle. Little after-school activities like that. Extracurriculars, you could call them." Taylor smiled humbly, arched his eyebrow, and cutely waggled his head.

"It is delightful to meet you," said the monk. "We have been so long awaiting your arrival. The seedlings yearn for the fall of the first rain."

213

Jasper studied the monk's face. Was it a trick of the wavering light, or when they were introduced, had the monk just shot Taylor Quizmo, Secret Agent, a look of hatred and disdain—and then covered it up quickly with a smile?

Jasper and Lily traded glances. They didn't like this at all.

"We may rest for several hours until dawn," said the monk. "We must be at the ferry by nine in the morning."

It was an awful night. They all huddled in the stone chamber. No one could sleep. Everyone was cold, and no one had any blankets. Drgnan and Jasper were both wearing shorts. Taylor Quizmo even took the sweater from around his shoulders and actually put it on.

Some of the refugees were crying. They looked accusingly at Lily, Jasper, Drgnan, Katie, Taylor, and the unnamed monk. Even though the members of the Resistance knew it was an accident that the Ministry of Silence had been led to their secret lair—still, they clearly couldn't help but think that if these foreigners hadn't stumbled in with their bratty ways, everyone would still be sleeping on goose-down mattresses around a courtyard fragrant with yellow blossoms.

Lily kept asking herself what she could have done differently. Jasper clearly was asking himself the same thing. They both longed to be home, with their parents, so they could tell them the whole story and ask what was right and what was wrong, and have someone say, *It's not your fault*, even if it was their fault. Even if they had made some stupid mistake that had brought the Ministry of Silence right to Drrok's rooftop.

So the wretched hours passed in the chilly chamber: water dripping, sewage gurgling, the kids tired and guilty, Bvletch missing, and the Resistance, Delaware's only hope for freedom and liberty, betrayed.

NIBBLES AND WORRY

"The kids are probably having a great time," said Mr. Gefelty.

No one answered him. Mr. Gefelty and his wife sat in the Dashes' ultramodern living room. The room was made of white concrete and glass. The three of them had been sitting there, waiting for news, for four hours, and they did not have anything left to say. Mrs. Dash had prepared some party food to eat while they waited for the phone to ring. The food sat on plates, untouched. It was a dismal gathering. In the background there was music, a Moog synthesizer fluting away with its bloops and bleeps while Mrs. Dash stared through the plate-glass windows into the night.

She was dressed in a pink skirt-suit, and her hair was carefully fixed in a bell. She had tried very hard to put herself together, but she was falling apart. The flowers were wilting in chrome vases on the counters and tabletops. For days she had not left the big house with its cold cubicles and its huge, pitiless plate-glass windows.

Dolores Dash had neither husband nor boyfriend. Jasper's father had been a beam of binary information transmitted from the region of the Horsehead Nebula. If there was a father, he was on another world.

Mrs. Dash had spent the last two days crying. She wished there was someone—human or alien—with whom she could share the worry about her son. Someone who would take her hand in his hand, or his tentacle, or his ratchety claw, and say gently, firmly, "Dolores—Dolores—everything is going to be all right."

Instead Mr. Gefelty unconvincingly said,

"Maybe the kids are someplace logical we haven't thought of yet."

"Ben," said Mrs. Gefelty, "you can keep telling yourself that, but I'm terrified. And I think Dolores is too."

Mr. Gefelty said, "They're probably up late somewhere, watching movies and doing Mad Libs."

His wife frowned at him and sighed. She picked at her pinkie nail with her thumbnail.

Dolores Dash stared down at the floor. By her elbow, the robotic table served more hors d'oeuvres. A platter of little beef Wellingtons rose up through a panel.

"Oh," said Mrs. Gefelty without enthusiasm. "Beef Wellingtons. Dolores, I hope you didn't go to any trouble, having us over."

On small tables around them were a platter of shrimp, uneaten, a cheese board with some crackers, a plate of deviled eggs with each egg in its own divot, a bowl of hot chicken dip, a bowl of hummus, some cut vegetables, some party wieners on toothpicks, some mini-meatballs, some cocktail mushrooms, a pot of fondue, a tray of asparagus rolls, a bowl of olives stuffed with cream cheese, and triangles of spanikopita. Mrs. Dash stared at them.

"No," she whispered almost too quietly to be heard. "No trouble at all."

Ben Gefelty looked around at the glistening piles of food. None of them were hungry. He said, "Well, we should probably go. We don't want to impose."

Dolores Dash nodded. She thought of her son's empty bedroom upstairs, the sheets still rumpled, the balsa-wood spaceship models standing on the shelves.

Mrs. Gefelty reached over and pressed Mrs. Dash's hand. "If the kids don't . . . if we haven't heard by tomorrow, we'll have you over for the day to wait."

Mrs. Dash looked at the Gefeltys. What she said was, "That would be lovely, Susan. I'll bring some deviled eggs." What she wanted to say was, *My boy was sent to me on a beam of light through all the lonely reaches of space, and he is all I love on this Earth.*

"Don't worry, Dolores," said Mr. Gefelty, standing. "Bick Mulligan's family are all on the police force. He's made a bunch of calls and there's an all-points bulletin out. Or whatever the police have these days. They have computers, you know. It's not like back in the day."

Mrs. Dash said, "That's wonderful. I'm sure he's got it under control." Her voice was flat and sad.

"Dolores?" said Mrs. Gefelty. "You don't sound so good. Are you holding up all right?"

What Mrs. Dash said was, "I'm fine, Susan. Thanks." What she wanted to say was, *I drive lonely country roads at night, longing for something to descend from the stars. I come to rest in cornfields and press my forehead against the cold glass of the windshield, praying I'll see lights above the rows, huge beetle eyes gazing softly out at me through the stalks.*

"So how does nine o'clock tomorrow morning sound for you to drop by?" Mrs. Gefelty asked. "None of us should be alone while we're waiting."

What Mrs. Dash said was, "Certainly. Nine o'clock sounds delightful." What she wanted to say was, *There is no time that is right to wait for news of tragedy.*

"You call us if you need anything, okay?" said Mrs. Gefelty.

What Mrs. Dash said was, "Thank you. That's very kind. Don't worry about me." And yet she wanted to cry to them, *I wait for the radiant vision of saucer ships and silver suits in my backyard; I wait for a man's voice, alien and yet familiar, to call across the static on the television set, which I leave tuned to dead channels; I long for the power outage, the whimpering dog, the whispering, gray bodies in the toolshed; I wait for the tractor beam to enfold me and lift me up above the Earth like an embrace.*

But what Mrs. Dash said was, "It's so nice of you both to visit me."

There was a humming noise, and the robot table, oblivious to the departure of guests, delivered a plate of nachos and watery salsa.

By the Light of His Teeth

In the dirty, gray streets of Wilmington, people shuffled to work. Factory whistles were blowing all over the city. Wearing long coats and flat caps, men and women trudged up the hills, coughing and wiping their eyes.

And forty or fifty feet below them, deep in an octagonal chamber in the sewers, the refugees huddled on the brick floor, shivering.

Katie and Drgnan squatted next to each other. They didn't hold hands again or talk about holding hands.

Katie couldn't figure out whether Drgnan knew how much she liked him. She couldn't guess exactly what he'd meant by taking her hand, back there in the courtyard. When she

looked at him, though, he turned to look at her, and he smiled, and his smile made her feel warm despite the cold. He did not speak, but wrapped his arms around his knees.

She smiled back.

Lily and Jasper sat across from them. During the night, Lily had lent the Boy Technonaut her sweater to put over his bare legs. She couldn't stand how cold he looked. He had finally fallen asleep with his head on her feet.

"Children?" said the monk they'd called Grzo's friend. "It is time to rise and walk." He was crouched next to them, his hands on his knees.

Jasper woke up. He and Lily exchanged glances and then stood.

"It is seven. The ferry sails at ten. We must be at the dock by nine, so that they can check our papers."

"We don't have papers," said Jasper.

"Some of us have learner's permits," said Taylor Quizmo.

Jasper pulled out his wallet and flipped through it. "I have some cards relating to inter-galactic organizations," he said. "Are those accepted?"

"You are minors," said the monk. "You will be covered by my forged papers. We are a school group going to New York City to take in a show."

"My learner's permit," Taylor insisted, "was issued specially. Usually they wouldn't give a learner's permit to someone my age."

"Very impressive," said the monk. "But the sweet, young soul shall allow me to continue. We must be at the dock at nine, and it is an hour-and-a-half walk through the tunnels to get there. So let us leave now. We cannot be late."

They said good-bye to the refugees.

Lily asked them, "Where will you go?"

"Drrok, the gardener, is gone," said one of the guards. "He was the leader of our band. We must mourn for him. Then we shall find another band of Resistance fighters to join."

"We're, um, sorry," said Lily. "That . . . your . . . house . . ." She couldn't bring herself to say any more.

The refugees looked at her with unhappy eyes. She was able to escape to her own home again; they were not.

"Good-bye," she said.

The monk opened a metal door into a tunnel and bowed.

Katie gasped. As the monk bowed, she saw he had a gun hidden under his jacket. He saw her staring at him and smiled.

Silently, gagging on fear, she followed the others as they all filed out.

The others hadn't seen the gun. But still, they were miserable.

They trooped, stooped, through corridors. The monk led the way. He had apparently memorized directions. He seemed to know his way very well.

Jasper watched the man's back. "I don't like this," Jasper muttered. "I don't like it one little bit."

"He seemed nice when he was with Grzo," whispered Drgnan. "Now, though, he does not have a look of trust and love on his face."

"Do you think he's even leading us to Brother Grzo?" whispered Lily.

The monk, who was carrying an industrial flashlight ten or fifteen feet in front of them, turned and said, "Of what do you whisper? We must hurry."

At about eight, they took a breather.

"I am uncertain of which way to go," said the monk. "If you, little brothers and sisters, will stay here for one solitary minute, I will run forward up both these two passages and determine which one is correct."

He bowed and stalked off.

Immediately after he'd gone, Lily whispered, "He could be setting something up. Like an ambush."

And then Katie said, "He has a gun. He has a gun hidden under his jacket. I saw it when he bowed."

Lily's blood ran cold. Jasper started to his feet, unable to remain sitting in the midst of so much dastardy.

For the first time, Lily saw a look of doubt and worry on Taylor Quizmo's face.

"What are we going to do?" said Lily.

"He's leading us into a trap," said Taylor. "I just know it."

"Alas," said Drgnan, "that one who traveled with us upon the high road should beat us with the walking stick we shared."

"Let's get up to the street," said Jasper. "We can find our way to the ferry landing ourselves up there. We'll get lost down here."

They heard footsteps. He was coming back.

"Let's go," said Taylor. He looked anxiously into the others' faces. Everyone weighed the best thing to do.

"If this is true, then he has a heavy chain upon his spirit," said Drgnan. "He betrayed Bvletch and betrayed the location of the safe house."

"He's coming," said Katie.

And so they ran—fleeing down the corridor the monk hadn't explored.

They sprinted as fast as they could.

Taylor had been using a flashlight built into his dental retainer, so he now led the way as they scampered down a side passage, wildly looking for a ladder that would lead up and out of the maze of sewers.

"Children!" the monk roared behind them. "Where—?"

The echoes shot and bounced and rebounded all around them, and so did the light: an arm there—a slice of shadow—legs—darkness—a bit of stair—"Don't trip!" (called by someone, couldn't tell who . . .)—a hole—pipes—more legs—Lily couldn't see who was in front of her—Drgnan's shaved head—then complete dark—

"Taylor!" yelled Katie. "Keep smiling! We can't see when you close your mouth!"

Taylor, his face in an awful grin, his cheeks

still glistening with the grease from last night's fries, kept running, his arms swinging in panic.

"Come back, children! You will regret this jog! It will be called a sad jog by you, in the days to come!"

Jumbled in the dark, they had no sense of which way to run. They caught glimpses of pipes and drops and corridors—but only glimpses.

The rogue monk had switched off his light. They could tell he was creeping through the dark, seeking them, and they couldn't see him.

Lily was last in line. She drew her arms in close to her. She felt like at any moment, she could be grabbed.

Taylor's dental light swooped through the cavernous darkness.

They were on a rickety little metal bridge over an underground river. They had reached a T and could go left or right. The iron bridge swayed and creaked as they looked at the two branches. They could no longer hear the monk pursuing them.

"Where is he?" Jasper asked.

"I don't know," said Katie. "Where are *we*?"

"We're lost," Lily lamented. "And the monk is behind us somewhere."

"There are times," said Taylor, between gritted teeth (he was smiling), "when you can't do something alone." He pulled out his cell phone and hit a number. Over the sound of churning water, the phone dialed.

Quickly, he shouted, "Hello—It's Taylor Quizmo, Secret Agent—I'm a friend of Senator Fairview's—sent to pick up these children—little kids—who . . . Okay. Okay. Yeah, there's a monk, a rogue monk—he has a gun—and he's chasing us through the sewers. Can you fix on my location? Okay? Can you get it? From the phone . . . ? Great! Now tell us how we can get out of here. You must have a computer screen with a map, and there we are . . . Yes? . . . That's us, blinking. Quickly: Where do we . . . ?"

It is lucky that Taylor Quizmo said a long letter *e* in "we." This is what allowed them all

to see that the nameless monk was standing on one side of the bridge, dressed in his T-shirt, jacket, and tracksuit bottoms. He was panting from the chase and holding his gun.

"Stop," he said. "Put the phone down. Put your hands up. And walk back this way. Slowly."

"RUN!" said Taylor Quizmo, and he shut his mouth and bolted.

Of course, everyone was happy that he had shut his mouth for several reasons, but mainly because it meant that the room was cast momentarily into darkness before the rogue monk switched his flashlight back on. He swatted the spot back and forth until he found Lily's heels, and then he took off after them, clanking across the bridge.

Taylor was getting directions through his cell phone. He led them up little staircases and down ramps.

Finally there was a long, long staircase going up.

"We're almost out!" said Taylor, and snapped his phone shut.

They all charged up the stairs.

Lily was falling behind. She could hardly see, since the only source of light was coming out of Taylor Quizmo's mouth, which was several mouths in front of hers. Katie slowed to urge her along.

The nameless monk was behind them. He shouted threats still, but they could no longer hear the words. There were too many echoes, too much of the crack of hard shoe heels on brick.

"Through here! We're free!" said Taylor, slamming a door open.

They ran through it—

Out into a dark room—vast by the sound of its echoes. They started to cross. . . .

Suddenly Lily realized there was a spotlight on them.

It was all she could see.

Them, surrounded by the light.

Taylor Quizmo had stopped running and looked around, gasping for breath.

Lily listened carefully. It sounded a little as if the room was full of hidden people waiting.

The nameless monk ran in behind them and skittered to a stop.

And a voice that Lily had never heard before—but which was the voice of the Governing Committee of Wilmington—hissed, "Super. I'm glad you could make it."

And with that, all the lights came on.

The Game Is Up

It was hard for the kids to figure out what was going on in the next few seconds. Why, for example, was a huge jazz band blaring out a tune in an orchestra pit? Why all the shrieking brass and the thrilling, trilling chords? Who could explain the rows of flashing lights, or the disco ball, or the man in a long black coat sitting on a high stone seat, wearing metallic mittens? What was the reason for the huge studio audience clapping, for the giant neon words in Doverian, for the beautiful women in glittering, sequined dresses coming forward to take the kids by the hand and lead them down to a row of reserved seats?

Why was a booming voice welcoming them, saying,

"IT'S TIME FOR EVERYONE'S FAVORITE SHOW!

IT'S TIME TO BE FROG-MARCHED DOWN MEMORY LANE— ON . . .

THIS . . . IS YOUR DOUBLE LIFE!!!"

It was the game show they'd watched earlier, in which the Autarch's spies were celebrated for their weaselly trickery, and enemies of the Delaware government were unmasked and punished—all in front of a studio audience.

And Lily, Katie, Jasper, Drgnan, and Taylor were apparently guest stars!

Lovely assistants of the State, as beautiful and inhuman as angels, sat the kids in their seats and pulled out guns to keep them quiet. Lily saw that Drrok and the other Resistance fighters who'd been taken by the Ministry were sitting right next to her, handcuffed, also guarded by beauties with lamé sheath dresses and pistols. On the backs of all their seats were taped colored pieces of paper that read RESERVED FOR POLITICAL PRISONERS.

So far as the kids could make it out, they were in some room in Wilmington Castle. They didn't know who the man on the granite throne to the side of the stage was—the pale man in the black coat and the iron mitts—but he seemed to be in charge.

There was only one person left on the stage itself.

The nameless monk.

He looked defiant and proud.

The man in the black coat rasped into a microphone, "Greetings, citizens. We are the Governing Committee of Wilmington. Welcome to our show. Are we going to have a great time today?" he asked the audience.

The crowd went crazy. Except for the people in the first couple of rows, who were all prisoners, and who didn't seem very jolly.

The rest of the studio audience was made up of the Autarch's own spies and informants. They got to come see the show as a special favor for turning people in. They clapped and yelled and crowed and hooted. The cameras would have swept thrillingly across the crowd, except that would have broadcasted the faces of all of the Autarch's most important spies and informants in Wilmington on TV for everybody to see, which would have been kind of a mistake.

If everyone knew they were spies, then they couldn't spy anymore. This is one of the problems with spy-based reality television.

So the audience (except for the political prisoners in the first two rows) all screamed with pleasure incognito, while a man in black held up a sign that said APPLAUSE! OR ELSE!

Finally the clapping died down.

"Welcome, citizens, to *This Is Your Double Life!*" said the Committee, "the show where we celebrate the Autarch's best spies and unmask enemies of the State. Who is who? Who is your friend and who is your foe? We reveal all.

"Today's guest appears to have just stumbled in." The Committee climbed down off his throne and walked to the side of the nameless monk. "It's delightful to have you here today," he said in his unhappy, hissing voice. "What's your name, citizen?"

The nameless monk didn't answer—just smiled gently.

"And where are you coming from today?"

"Vbngoom," the monk answered. "The Platter of Heaven."

"Wonderful. Super," said the Committee. "Now where are you really from?"

The monk didn't answer.

Katie whispered to Lily, "What's going on?"

"I think," Lily whispered back, "that Grzo's friend is about to be, you know, congratulated for turning all of us in. On daytime television."

The Committee was pacing around onstage, grimacing. "Let's have a volunteer from the audience," he hissed. "Someone from the first two rows. The political prisoners who have been kind enough to join us today. Anyone?" No one around Lily raised their hands. For one thing, most of them had on handcuffs. The Committee barked, "You, citizen!" He pointed.

Drrok was hauled up out of his seat. He was forced up onstage.

The Committee addressed him: "And you are called?"

"The gardener."

"Drrok, the gardener," announced the Committee. "Leader of a resistance group in Wilmington. Let us hear it for Drrok, the gardener, citizens."

The crowd of spies and informants went wild, booing and hissing. It took a long time for them to quiet down, even when the Committee gestured for silence with his big, mittened hands.

When it was quiet, he said to Drrok, "Look at this monk, citizen Drrok. Friend or foe, that is the question. Friend or foe? Consider that he may have passed directions to your HQ along to me and my espionage unit. Do you have anything to say to him, sir? Anything angry and cruel? We love anger and accusations here at the Castle."

Drrok stood proudly and defiantly beneath the lights.

"Is it possible," said Drrok to the nameless monk, "that you sold us all to the Ministry of

Silence? We had a home, where we played upon our instruments and sang of ancient sadnesses. We tended our garden and prepared for the day when the Governor of Delaware shall return to rule the Blue Hen State, and shall sit again upon the Chicken Throne—"

"All right," rasped the Committee. "Less about the Governor. More about your anger at being betrayed. Any response, my monkish friend?"

"You know my—"

"Another volunteer from the audience!" said the Committee. He did not wait for hands to go up. He jabbed a scrawny finger. "Him!"

Drgnan was pulled to his feet. The women pushed him up the steps onto the stage.

"Your name, boy?"

"Brother Drgnan Pghlik."

"Citizens, I give you—Brother Drgnan Pghlik," crowed the Committee.

The crowd of enemy spies hissed and screamed. Drgnan bowed his head.

The Committee asked him, "Do you have anything to say to this man?"

With sorrowful dignity, Drgnan Pghlik told the nameless monk, "If you betrayed our order and led us to this indignity, then your sadness should be even greater than my own. Our order is all that brings me joy, and this is true for many. We supply help to others and seek to—"

"Fine!" said the Committee. "Gut-wrenching. How do you feel, having let these people down?" he asked the nameless monk.

"I didn't think that—"

"He didn't think!" announced the Committee. "He admits he didn't think. But is he friend or is he foe? Enemy of the State or espionage asset for our glorious Autarch? But first, more from his fellow prisoners." The Committee growled, "And now . . . we shall welcome to the stage . . . you, young sir." He was pointing at Taylor Quizmo.

Taylor swaggered up onto the stage. He was

smiling and chewing a wad of Chiclets. While the music played for his entrance, he waved and winked at the audience.

"Your name, citizen?"

"Taylor Quizmo, Secret Agent."

"And perhaps you will tell us, Taylor Quizmo, your story?"

Taylor Quizmo picked up the microphone like he was about to sing. He crinkled up his eyes and said, "Let me say first how glad I am to be here. It's a real pleasure to be here in the Castle tonight. Thanks to the Governing Committee of Wilmington for inviting me and my friends. We're so grateful."

"It was nothing," hissed the Committee. "We wouldn't have had it any other way."

"You know," said Taylor, giving his most winning smile to the cameras, "I'm not from Delaware, but I feel like a Delawarian. I love this state. It's a beautiful state, isn't it? Isn't it?"

The crowd went wild with yes. Taylor was a natural on television.

"I love the Blue Hen State!" he cried, raising his arm.

Everyone was cheering. Taylor waved and grinned. The band played a few bars of "Fair Delaware." The crowd was loud.

"Very kind of the prisoner, we're sure," said the Committee. "Perhaps, however, the prisoner would be so good as to tell us his story?"

"Sure!" Taylor Quizmo's gum cracked. He paced back and forth, the microphone cord snaking along behind him, flipping over, coming to rest. Taylor said, "A few days ago I got word that the monks of Vbngoom were sending a van north from their hidden mountain, whatever, and that three kids from another state were with them, and that they were going to cross the border into Pennsylvania or New Jersey so they could try to get back some sacred doodads. And I heard that Control, the head of the Ministry of Silence, was planning on stopping these kids and these monks when they crossed the border. He was going to have

them questioned so he could figure out where they were keeping the Monastery of Vbngoom. He was making a big deal about it. Security was stepped up all along the border, at each of the major checkpoints, and there were spies all up and down the roads, looking for the kids and the van. And I realized—it's time for Taylor Quizmo, Secret Agent."

"Indeed, citizen," said the Committee.

"I realized—these kids are going to escape if I don't lend a hand. You know, that's why Control called me and not someone else. Because he knows that Taylor Quizmo gets things done. He knows that Taylor Quizmo, Secret Agent, always nabs his man. So Control gave me a cell phone with a tracer chip in it, and some poison darts—he always gives me some pretty cool gear—and . . ."

Lily couldn't hear any more. There was a rushing noise in her ears. She was thinking a mile a minute . . . because *Taylor Quizmo was an enemy spy.*

Lily gasped. It hadn't been Bvletch who had given away the position of the safe house. It hadn't been some snooping spy hiding in a mailbox. It hadn't been the nameless monk. It had been Taylor himself.

Now that she thought about it, it made perfect sense. When he appeared by the hay cart to help them, he had just *pretended* to help—letting the Ministry of Silence drag Bvletch away. Taylor needed Lily and her friends to trust him so they'd lead him to the secret hideout.

And then she realized: How had he gotten his Hummer so close to the spot where he met them when he couldn't drive it without an adult? *Someone* must have driven with him and helped him parallel park it . . . someone from the Ministry of Silence.

And she remembered that Taylor had gotten a cell phone call at the safe house just before the attack. Probably it had been the Committee's henchmen, telling him to watch out for crossbow bolts.

And when they were lost in the tunnels under the city, Taylor had called someone—probably a servant of the Ministry of Silence—and had gotten instructions on how to get them into the Castle's theater. Taylor Quizmo knew that he was leading them all into a trap! He wasn't the real U.S. spy after all!

The REAL U.S. spy, Lily realized, *the real U.S. spy was the NAMELESS MONK!* That's why the nameless monk had just joined the monastery of Vbngoom! He wasn't a monk at all! In the tunnels, he'd been trying to stop and disarm the actual traitor . . . Taylor Quizmo. He'd been trying to warn her and her friends.

Lily looked down dolefully into her lap.

The Committee said to Taylor, "So, Taylor Quizmo, you betrayed them all?"

Taylor grinned. "Anything for the fabulous *Ministry of Silence*!" He spread his arms generously.

The crowd of informers and stooges went wild.

"Seriously," said Taylor. "I may be from DC, but I love you Delaware guys."

"Foolish boy!" cried the nameless monk. "Oh, foolish, foolish boy! You do not know what suffering you've caused!"

"Hey, it's better than a paper route." He winked at the crowd and got a big laugh.

"You'll never get away with this!" the monk swore.

"That's what your type always says." Taylor jabbed his thumb toward the nameless monk. He asked the crowd, "Is he the best the United States government could drum up?" The audience laughed again.

"My *type*?" said the nameless monk. "I am a public servant of the United States! And no little cub like you is going to stop us from seeing that justice is done!"

"Sorry, pops," said Taylor Quizmo, his eyes getting narrow and mean. "It looks like I already have. Justice is for the strong."

"You'll never—"

249

"This is all very sweet," hissed the Committee. "Very lovely. Great entertainment." To the audience, he growled, "So now you have it, my lovely horde of baying lapdogs and lickspittles: The lid is off! The tripes are exposed! Taylor Quizmo is our beloved Autarch's spy, and this nameless monk, this wretched fool, is the intruder, sent here to aid the Resistance and the Monastery of Vbngoom. These prisoners in the front row, these kids, befriended their enemy, betrayed their friends, and ran from their ally. But now we know who is who. Now we know who loves our glorious State, and who seeks stupidly to overthrow it. There we have it. Done." The Committee paused and cleared his throat. He rasped, "So now . . . now it is everyone's favorite part of the show: the part where we punish and destroy."

All the spies in the audience went crazy. They were clapping and cheering.

Lily felt the disaster in every part of her. The Committee of Wilmington's words echoed in her ears: *befriended their enemy, betrayed their friends, and ran from their ally.* They had been stupid. And now . . . she didn't even want to think. She felt sick. Panicked. Frightened.

The women in glittering dresses gestured. All the prisoners—Katie, Lily, Jasper, the shackled members of the Resistance—all of them were led up onstage and put next to Drgnan and Drrok. Lily looked around, desperate—there must be some hope.

But all she saw were the cruel faces in the audience, the jeering of people willing to betray their friends and their country.

Jasper was wide eyed with rage and worry. He couldn't believe that anyone would be so villainous—and that the End might be Nigh.

"Now," the Committee was saying, "I'm an old-fashioned man. And there's nothing that says 'old-fashioned' to a spy like a shark pit. Lights, Ghty!"

A spotlight hit right near the prisoners' feet. It shone through the floor. Below, through frosted glass, the kids could see sharks nipping and spinning.

Lily was shaking with fear. Katie and Drgnan exchanged panicked looks. Jasper prepared for punching.

"And, to drop them in," said the Committee, "to send them to their gory doom, we have none other than a recent convert to the Autarch's ranks . . . someone who, after a little session with me in a tricky little room with lots of nasty little devices, saw the light and decided to join our side . . ."

There was a drumroll.

"And his name is: BVLETCH!"

REALDOM

Forth came Brother Bvletch from the wings, his shoulders sagging, his pimples glistening in the swirling spotlights. His eyes were glazed. He looked like a zombie.

"Brother Bvletch!" said Drgnan in despair. "Bvletch!"

Bvletch did not seem to see anyone. He walked like a robot over to the Governing Committee. The Committee held out a metal mitt, and Bvletch shook it.

"Welcome!" rasped the Committee. "Welcome, young Bvletch."

"It is great to be here," said Bvletch in an automatic voice.

"Now, tell me, Bvletch, you were a monk

253

of Vbngoom. But you had a little talk with me yesterday evening. How did you enjoy our little talk?"

"I wish it could have gone on all night, until the morning star faded and the moon sank beneath the brow of the hills."

"And now that we've had our little talk, how do you feel about our glorious warlord, the Awful and Adorable Autarch of Dagsboro?"

"He is a great guy," said Bvletch without any enthusiasm, staring straight ahead. "It would be great to be his friend. I dream that I could go over to his house and watch a game on the television while sharing a bowl of mixed nuts."

"We all can dream, Citizen Bvletch, can't we? We all can dream."

"It would be awesome."

"Awesome indeed, citizen. Now, what are you looking forward to, Citizen Bvletch? What would you like to do more than anything else right now?"

"You know what would be great, sir?" said Bvletch, in a voice that sounded like a recording. (His eyes were still blank.)

"What would be great, young fellow?"

"I would like to drop my friends and the members of the Resistance into a shark tank."

"With a lever?"

"However you tell me to, sir."

"Lovely. Because, Bvletch . . . we just happen to have a shark tank . . . and your friends . . . and a lever."

"And a lever, sir?" said Bvletch. He droned, "This is more wonderful than I ever could have imagined."

"Splendid, citizen," hissed the Committee. He clapped his hands, and the brass blew a screaming jazz fanfare. A panel in the wall dropped open, revealing a giant red lever.

The Committee led Bvletch over to the lever. He put the teen's hand on it.

"One yank of this lever," said the Committee, "will send all your friends and the Resistance

fighters into the drink. And it is a drink with some nasty little fixin's in it, citizen." The Committee beckoned to a cameraman. "Traitor-cam, roll over here. We want to see every twitch of this young man's face as he sends his friends to their deaths." The cameraman slid his cam forward to get a close-up. As he did so, the Committee explained to the prisoners, "You should all know that this boy has, you might say, spilled all the beans. He has told us about how Vbngoom has moved. Yes, well might you look shocked, young monk!"

Drgnan Pghlik made a sound of woe.

"Yes, Citizen Pghlik. He told us that—and even told us generally where it went: the mountains in the far south, below Seaford."

Far south? Lily thought to herself. *Wait—Vbngoom went northwest. But then why didn't Bvletch . . . ?*

And she saw: Bvletch hadn't been converted at all! He hadn't told the Committee anything! *He had talked entirely in irony! He had said the opposite of what he meant! Just like his Vow of Sarcasm demanded! And he was still talking in irony!*

The Committee sneered, "The monks of Vbngoom cannot lie—and so I know that every word that fell from this youth's lips is truth. And did he talk? He did. At length. And he told us about the pitiful Resistance. He told us you're planning attacks on zebra-back. Lady musketeers on zebra-back—isn't that right? Hear me and despair! He told us about your submarines that go through the dirt! He explained about the secret cameras in breakfast cereal! He told me about the detachable teeth, the special fries, your life in soup, the wig contests! And he gave me the name of the leader of the Resistance—not simply Citizen Drrok here, but the leader of the whole movement in Delaware: a woman named Citizen Realdom. Isn't that right?"

"You have got that right, sir," said Bvletch.

"I. M. Realdom," said the Committee in

dolorous glee. "That is the name. I am not afraid to say it on television. I. M. Realdom—beware! All will seek you out now and destroy you. Do you hear me, Citizen Realdom? *Who do we seek, my spies?* Again and again, I announce to the world: I. M. Realdom! I. M. Realdom! I. M. Realdom! I cannot say it too often! Do you have that?"

"I bet they hear it loud and clear, sir, like the dripping of water into a still forest pool."

"And now," croaked the Committee. "Now it is time, Citizen Bvletch, to prove your loyalty to the Autarch!"

For the first time, Lily saw Bvletch twitch.

"You shall either drop your friends into the tank—or join them. Traitor-cam, get that expression. I like the pain and confusion."

The band played. Lights flashed on and off around the perimeter of the shark tank. The kids looked down and saw the floor that was about to drop them. They saw the sharks roiling.

Nearby, on the edge of the stage, Taylor was sharing his Chiclets with one of the lovely female spies.

Lily watched Bvletch in terror—watched his face as he tried to make a decision between dropping his friends into a shark tank and dropping his disguise.

Lily didn't see how anyone was going to make it out of this alive. She and Katie clamped hands. Katie was crying. She wiped away the tear with her wrist.

"Is everyone ready?" the Committee called in his gravelly voice.

The crowd was going completely crazy. About twenty people were about to be fed to sharks.

"Are *you* ready, Citizen Bvletch?"

Bvletch was looking around. He was realizing that it was do or die. He didn't want to die, and he didn't know what to do.

He looked around, blinking.

The camera moved toward him. His face,

warped with confusion, appeared on a giant screen behind him. His doubt was huge.

"Pull the lever," said the Committee. "Pull it now."

And Bvletch reached up with his hand to yank.

The band blasted a swing tune. Lights zipped up and down the aisles, along the edge of the stage, overhead, and the tank-cam showed the sharks chomping their teeth in readiness.

Bvletch stood, miserable, his acne glowing like the fairground lights around him.

The Committee watched him.

The traitor-cam showed Bvletch's doubt.

The Committee raised a mittened hand. . . .

And then Bvletch launched himself onto the television camera right in front of him. He jumped and grabbed and the camera rolled backward, knocking over the technician, skidding toward the edge of the stage. Bvletch swiveled the lens toward the audience, and as everyone erupted into screams, he himself yelled into the microphone, "Real great audience, super audience—see, Greater Wilmington?—super!—SPIES! ALL OF THEM! YOUR FRIENDS AND NEIGHBORS! GREAT PEOPLE! REALLY TRUSTWORTHY! SEE THEIR FACES? AREN'T THEY SUPER? DON'T YOU LOVE THEM? AREN'T YOU GLAD YOU'RE THEIR FRIENDS?" The spies in the audience were diving for the floor. They couldn't be seen, or everyone would know that they were informing, turning people in to the Ministry of Silence—and so they panicked and plunged down behind their chairs or stampeded up the aisles. There were fruit sellers and fish sellers and grannies and old men and little rope-jumping girls—all of them instantly broadcasted to every television set in Wilmington—so everyone knew who was secretly skulking for the Autarch.

And in that moment of confusion, everything went haywire: Folding chairs clattered.

The Committee bellowed. The gorgeous assistant assassins went karate on the Resistance! The Resistance blocked and smacked with blistered wrists. Dazzle was everywhere. The band played on. Lily grabbed Katie and squatted her down low so they wouldn't be hit by stray punches. Katie was still stunned by events and bewildered. Over the screaming, Lily shouted the news that Bvletch had been sarcastic.

Drgnan and Jasper were doing a little move to knock out slinky spyettes in glittering dresses: Jasper picked up Drgnan and spun him so he flew off the ground—Drgnan kicked, knocked out a gal with a pistol, and landed on his feet in time to swing and lift Jasper—who scissored his legs, whopped a chick's crossbow out of her hands, and skated to his feet so he could twirl Drgnan—and they made a slow progress through the security babes trying to catch hold of them.

The stage was crowded with fighting. The

audience was emptying. People were fleeing for the exits. Bvletch was still holding on to the back of the camera, broadcasting the faces of informants as Drrok, the gardener, held off the director of photography, who hurled himself at Bvletch in an attempt to protect his own life and his ratings.

Drgnan and Jasper had reached the edge of the ring of guards when they ran into Taylor Quizmo, Secret Agent, who was trying to kayo Resistance fighters with darts from his cell phone.

"You betrayed us and the safe house that took us in," said Drgnan.

"And you are unsportsmanlike," said Jasper.

"Cry me a river, dudes," said Taylor, and raised his thumb to punch a button.

With that, the three set to fighting. Drgnan lashed out with his foot to knock the cell phone out of Taylor's hand—only to be struck by a dart himself.

Taylor exclaimed with pleasure as Drgnan yelped. The boy spy aimed for Jasper. Jasper grabbed Taylor's wrist. Grunting, Jasper steered the business end of the phone away from his face. Taylor stomped at Jasper's feet. Drgnan reeled from the knockout drug on the dart.

"You'll never succeed," said Jasper. "Democracy always wins in the end."

"You'll enjoy a nice long stay in Fort Delaware," Taylor replied. "By the time you get out, your stupid books will be another forty years out of date."

He lunged—and Jasper saw what Taylor was grabbing for: the lever that would dump everyone in the center of the stage into the shark tank!

He was desperate. Drgnan was knocked cold now, crumpled on the floor. Jasper had to stop the crazed secret agent from pulling that lever, or many of the Resistance (and some of the Ministry of Silence's guards, at this point!) would be dumped into the drink.

Jasper struggled. Taylor turned toward him—opened his mouth—and dazzled Jasper for an instant with his retainer light.

Then he reached for that fatal lever.

And he would have pulled it too, if Lily hadn't grabbed his ankle and yanked. Taylor fell, and Jasper pounced on him in an instant, grabbing the kid's shirtfront and declaring, "It is time for evil to say, 'Uncle!' Or 'Pax!' Or whatever it is fellows say nowadays when you've lost at fisticuffs fair and square, and you want to shake hands like men and end a dustup."

Taylor started crying with rage. His face was red, and he kept his hand outstretched toward the lever like a baby toward its bottle.

So went the fighting.

But most important, in the middle of all this chaos, was a little struggle going on by the back wall of the stage. Two men.

The unnamed monk and the skinny Committee of Wilmington.

The monk was trained to fight and capture, being a secret agent. The Committee of Wilmington was not.

"Let go of us, citizen!" hissed the Committee. "Or you shall feel the wrath of our iron fists!"

"Is that iron?" said the unnamed monk. "The pom-poms look more like brass."

"Yes, all right, fine, the pom-poms are brass. But my grip is iron."

"Lily," called the unnamed monk. "Lily, get me a microphone."

Lily ran, ducking, through the battle, and picked up the mike from the floor. She rushed it to the unnamed monk and held it toward his mouth.

"TESTING!" he shouted.

Everyone shut up.

And the unnamed monk, holding the Committee in a clinch with one arm, declared loudly, to the echoing room, "I ARREST THE GOVERNING COMMITTEE OF WILMING-

TON IN THE NAME OF THE LAW! *ALL*
THE MEMBERS OF THE COMMITTEE!"

"STOP!" said one of the female assassins.
"Let the Committee go! We're aiming right at
you, secret agent!" She pointed her gun.

The unnamed monk swiveled. "I wouldn't
do that, ladies," he said. "You'll hit the Committee. And he's legally under arrest. You'd
better start making arrangements for us to get
out of this Castle."

Everyone stood in confusion. No one really
knew what to do. It was kind of unclear who
was winning.

People looked around. They totted up a
score in their heads. I often have to do this
too, because I think fights are boring, and it
bugs me that people think problems can be
solved with a stupid one-two punch and a nest
of sharks.

People who looked around saw that the
Resistance had done a pretty good job of freeing
themselves from their guards. People saw that

Jasper was sitting on top of Taylor Quizmo, arms crossed, waiting for the boy spy to admit that he had lost fairly in a fight. Bvletch, of course, had broadcast the identity of most of the Ministry of Silence's operatives in Wilmington. Most of those double-crossers had run away. And even though many of the guard women in their cocktail glitter dresses were still standing, the unnamed monk had really gotten the better of the vile Governing Committee.

As if to underline the final point, the unnamed monk declared, "THE GOVERN-ING COMMITTEE OF WILMINGTON IS HEREBY SUSPENDED FROM ITS DUTIES AS THE RULING BODY OF THIS CITY UNTIL FURTHER NOTICE!"

There was an instant of confusion. Then almost everyone cheered. Freedom! They were all leaving the Castle! They were all going home. The prisoners would be freed; the crazy Committee would never rule there again.

Some of the guards and goons looked frustrated, but there wasn't much they could do. If they fired on the unnamed monk, they'd hit the arrested Committee.

The nameless monk asked, into the microphone, "Will the band please play a little something to celebrate the arrest? For freedom, my friends—freedom deserves a louder fanfare than tyranny!"

"Don't play anything!" hissed the Committee. "I command you, citizens!"

"Committee, you have the right to remain silent," said the secret agent monk. "And I really wish you would."

The band struck up the *Fanfare for the Common Man*, but with swing. "Wow!" said Katie, looking longingly at the snoozing Drgnan. "It kind of makes you want to dance."

The nameless monk said, "Freedom always makes you want to dance."

Jasper agreed sternly, "There's nothing like a waltz with Lady Liberty." Contentedly he batted away Taylor Quizmo's prying fingers, which were trying to gouge at his eyes.

"When you dance with democracy," said the nameless monk, "you dance with millions."

The Committee grumped, "All those feet get in the way. . . . There's much less tripping when there's only one man onstage and the audience is in the dark."

"But now the spotlight of justice," said the monk, "is burning through the—"

"Hey!" said Katie. "Hey!" And when they stared at her: "Um, don't we have a ferry to catch?"

And she was right.

It was time to go home at last.

Anchorites Away!

They were allowed out of the Castle without resistance. None of the guards or soldiers wanted to risk harming the grim-faced Committee.

It was a big crowd of them: the nameless monk, Lily, Jasper, Katie, Drgnan Pghlik, Bvletch, Drrok, about twenty men and women of the Resistance, and assorted other political prisoners who they released from the dungeons. They walked right out the front gates of the Castle, through the portcullis. The morning air was bright and blue.

The nameless monk was looking around suspiciously, worried about how they were going to get down to the docks. But he needn't have worried.

Because all over the city, a daytime fiesta was going on. Everyone had seen *This Is Your Double Life!* They'd seen the bad spies unmasked and the Committee arrested. The Autarch's authority in Wilmington—at least for the moment—was broken. And so everyone was celebrating in the streets.*

There was the sound of music—Delawarian rock from boom boxes and old tunes from street-side fiddlers and accordion players—and there was cheering. As soon as the band of prisoners strolled out of the gates, people in nearby apartments began to whistle and hoot and clap.

The unnamed monk and his charges hadn't walked far before an ancient festival cart pulled up, carved with the face of some mountain-squid god, pulled by four oxen. The citizens around it gestured for the kids to get in, so they could be whisked to the boat.

---

*Taylor Quizmo, on the other hand, had somehow gotten away in the confusion. He's probably gone for good. I don't suppose he'll ever return in a sequel when our friends least expect him.

They tied the Committee up in the front. He was off to face trial in Washington, DC. He sat grimly in his ropes, scowling.

The others climbed on the cart. The nameless monk and the kids said a fond farewell to Drrok.

Lily said to him, "I'm sorry that we brought Taylor Quizmo to your house. We endangered you all. I feel awful."

Drrok shook his head. "Dearest girl, the gods arrange all. Yes, we lost our house, but now the spies of Wilmington have been unmasked—and the Committee is no more."

"I am too 'more,'" rasped the Committee.

"You have done us a great service," said Drrok to Lily. "And we shall one day do such a service for you."

He bowed, putting his hands over his eyes, in the Delawarian gesture of respect.

Lily bowed in the same way, and they parted friends.

The ceremonial cart rumbled over the dirt

roads down the hill toward the mighty Delaware River. Katie spent the time fawning over Drgnan, who was just waking up. Jasper sat up in the front of the cart with the nameless monk and the Committee, talking shop. And Lily spent these minutes catching her final glimpses of the magical land of Delaware—drinking in the strangeness and the antiqueness she had come to love.

She saw the dry fountains, the old rows of Baroque houses, the puttering diesel trucks. She saw the people tumbling out of the factories to see their oppressor, the Committee, hauled out of his roost for the first time in decades. They laughed and waved. Where there had been only frowns before, now there were smiles.

It is a dream, that any place could be transformed like this, but it is not a bad dream to keep in mind. Although it may be impossible in any realm outside of that most mystic of mid-Atlantic states, this is what we need to wish for.

Of course, there was still hardship in the world: The Autarch still ruled, and he would doubtless send some other servant to take over the city. But by then the Resistance would be dug in deeper and would have created even more places where people could hide and be happy. They would strengthen themselves and gain allies and prepare for the glorious day when they might rise up and replace His Despotic Highness with the truly elected Governor once more, and with that shining figure sitting upon the Chicken Throne of the Blue Hen State, the throne of gold and lapis lazuli, the whole land might feel this happiness.

Do not dismiss moments of triumph just because sorrow might follow. Sure, after joy, sorrow comes. But after years of sorrow, joy comes too.

And at ten, the ferry came, and joyfully, the kids, the secret agent monk, and their prisoner got aboard. They met Brother Grzo, who was waiting for them with the van. It was already parked in the hold of the ferry with the other vehicles.

They went up and got a table on the upper deck, near the snack bar. Lily said she would take orders for food, since they hadn't had any breakfast. She patiently wrote them all down, even when the Committee kept on demanding different fixin's on his foot-long hot dog.

"Take your last look at Wilmington," said the secret agent.

"I cannot bear to see the city I ruled so long and so well for the last time," said the Committee, "while I am sitting next to a 'snack bar.' I, who am accustomed to hear screams for mercy, listening instead to the growling of the slushie machine. This is no way for a despot to travel."

"Beatific children," said Brother Grzo, "I am so pleased we are together again. My heart broke when I heard that the safe house had been raided."

"We were very worried," said the unnamed monk.

Jasper asked, "Brother Grzo, did you know that . . ."—he pointed at the monk—"that this gentleman was the U.S. spy we were waiting for?"

Grzo smiled and admitted, "It was my suspicion from the start. I had almost no doubt. But I could not be told, because then I could not have practiced deception, and I would have given him away."

"What is your name, actually?" Katie asked.

The nameless monk shrugged. "I have no name in Delaware. In the other states, I am just called O. That is my secret name. Agent O. But because of the lack of vowels in Delaware, when I am there, I am named by no letter at all."

"Aha!" said Katie. "It all makes perfect sense."

"No, it does not," Jasper said sternly. "We were told by the waiter to look for an Agent Q, not an Agent O. He wrote a Q on Grzo's drinking glass with his finger."

"Not precisely," said Agent O. "The waiter wrote an O. When Grzo picked the glass up and turned it around, his fingerprint made the

O into a *Q*. I saw the error, but could not speak of it for fear I would give my identity away."

"Wow," said Katie. "Because of that *Q*, we thought Taylor Quizmo was our spy guide." She shook her head, her mouth open. "It's amazing what a difference a little fingerprint can make."

Grzo agreed, "Wise words, my child."

"So now," said Agent O, "we'll drop off the Committee with the FBI agents we'll meet on the other shore. Then we'll go pick up your monastery's sacred objects—"

"And drop off the beautiful children at their homes," said Grzo.

"And then we'll come back to Delaware so we can return to Vbngoom."

Brother Grzo looked delighted. "You are returning to Vbngoom?"

Agent O nodded. "I love Vbngoom," he said. "I would like to become a monk there for real, and help in the fight against the Autarch. For many years I have been undercover in one disguise or another, working with the Delaware

Resistance. Now I would like to make my disguise reality. And reality disguise."

"Ah!" said Brother Grzo, clapping his hands to his forehead. "I can tell already that you shall go far in monkery! Disguise! Reality! An abbot of our order could not have said it more confusingly!"

"Since we speak of our vows and our order," said Drgnan Pghlik, "I believe we should all incline our heads to Bvletch, who did not falter in his strong work of sarcasm even when in the den of the enemy."

"Bvletch, my son," exclaimed Grzo, "you are a wonder!"

Bvletch blushed. He looked proudly down at his knees. "It was fun," he said. "I'd love to do it again."

"This is very ssssweet, citizens," grumbled the Committee, "but where's my foot-long?"

Meanwhile, the seagulls were crying over the water, and the boat was pulling away from the shores of Delaware.

Lily, waiting in line, looked out the window—a last glimpse. She saw the tugs and the old purple-sailed galleons. She saw the crowds in their *blrga* shirts and *pochbtvms.* She felt sorry to be leaving.

At the table, Drgnan said, "So now I shall see your home."

Jasper, assuming Drgnan was talking to him, said, "Yes, indeed. My mother will be very glad to have you as a guest."

Katie sighed with contentment, because she suspected that Drgnan was also excited to see the place she lived. She wondered what lay ahead for all of them.

A whistle blew. Jasper looked about and said, "Chaps, we are now all home free. We have pulled away from the shore."

"Yes, indeed," said Agent O. He pointed. "It is not long before we are at the middle of the river, and out of the jurisdiction of the Autarch. No one can stop us now."

"Unless," joked Katie, "there were one of those things like in a James Bond movie, and after you think you've defeated everyone, there's one spy left who puts up a little fight in the last chapter."

"No," said the table, shrugging their weight off his shoulders and standing up. "No, even I do not have such heart to fight on." He crossed his arms and looked wistfully back across the river.

Needless to say, it was Mrglik. Delaware's leading furniture-imitating spy.

"Bntno, he is down in automo-car waiting for a chase, yes? But why, I ask? We could fight, smack-smick, here. And you punch, and me punch."

"And I'd throw the food on you from behind," said Lily, coming up with the lunches.

"And Mr. Committee would run down the steps with his coat a-flap-flap," said Mrglik wearily. "And then he into the automo-car with Bntno. And they start the car up."

"But there's no place to go, since we're on a ferry," said Jasper.

"Exact. So then, if we can get car out, then we both drive—you drive in you van, Bntno drive in him automo-car—have very slow car chase, three mile per hour, in circles around boat. Maybe we get tired, stop to get out and have a slushie. Then get back in, keep up chase. But for what?"

"Who would really be chasing who?" asked Agent O. "When you're both chasing in a circle?"

("Ah!" crowed Brother Grzo, clapping. "Brother! By Saint Lrtguzl's bones! You were *made* to be a monk!")

Mrglik said dolorously, "We could have such chase."

"That sounds great," said Bvletch. "Like just what we want to do right now."

"No," said Mrglik. "No, no chase. What would be win? What would be lose? I call it even if you gets me a fish sandwich."

"Sure," said Lily.

"And for Bntno, some Jolly Ranchers."

"It's a deal," said Lily, smiling.

"I'd offer you a seat," said Katie, "but it might be one of your relatives."

"No, no seat," said Mrglik, waving his hand faintly. "I go rest by that binnacle there. Much to learn from that binnacle." He twisted up his mouth in some private sorrow. He said to them all, "So. We meet again, and yes, all that."

Then he clumped off with his huge Formica tabletop on his back. He sat by the binnacle and made a study of its rivets.

They were at the middle of the Delaware River. It was strange, but now when they looked back over the water, there was a funny kind of haze. They couldn't quite make out Wilmington anymore. Or at least, they couldn't see the Castle anymore. It was almost as if there weren't any Castle there at all. They could no longer see the sailing ships in the harbor. Just normal streets and houses. Power lines.

And then they were in New Jersey.

When they got off the ferry, there were two FBI agents waiting to take the Committee away. He hissed and glowered, but there was nothing he could do.

The friends looked for Mrglik, but he was nowhere to be seen.

As they got into the van, they saw Bntno in his car. He waved to them in a friendly kind of way, and opened up his mouth and stuck out his tongue to show them that a Jolly Rancher had turned it blue.

He didn't get off the ferry, but headed right back to Delaware.

The monks donned again their monkish robes, the green of Vbngoom. They and the kids got in the van and started driving.

They drove for hours. They drove past New York City, and Brother Drgnan's eyes were huge. He had never seen so many buildings, so many people. And he could not believe when they had traveled farther even than that—well into Connecticut—and still the sprawl continued. "It is the most amazing city I have ever seen!" he said. "It is like no place in Delaware!"

"It isn't the same city," Katie explained. "These places all have different names."

"But it all looks like one city," said Drgnan. "It is miraculous—it is like you people of the other states have made all places one. Truly, this is a marvel."

Katie grinned. "I'm glad you like it," she said.

"All of the houses, they are similar, and the stores, they are similar, and the roads—I cannot tell one from another. You see, to me, this is like nothing I have ever seen. To see it all spread like this for miles and miles and miles. I am filled with such joy."

"Cool," said Katie.

"Oh," said Drgnan, gripping the window's rubber seal, "if Rhode Island is exactly the same as Connecticut, with these same houses and roads and stores, I shall burst!"

"You can bet on it," said Katie. "It doesn't stop: It just gets thicker and thinner."

Lily was not quite so sure that she was glad to

be back in the midst of all the towns that looked identical from the highways, all the supermarkets laid out the same way, the stores that sold the same old pants. She already missed the smell of spices and the bleating of livestock, the danger of dragons and bears.

But also, she knew from having been to Delaware that in each one of these identical houses was a strange world too, with people as various as those who lined the market stalls of Dover. In these homes there were collections of butterflies mounted on boards, and there were women who spent their nights calling bakeries to check on orders they'd never left. There were children who ran multimillion-dollar businesses over the Internet, and dogs asleep, dreaming of pork chops the size of Stonehenge, and people of different religions who lit candles in their dining rooms to pray that they would never again be apart from those they loved. Best friends were sitting under trees as night fell, and in some room, a girl was lying on her bed, staring at her posters, in love with a boy who didn't know she existed.

Lily wondered what kind of adventures they would have now. Drgnan would be staying with Jasper for a while, and Lily had no doubt that all four of them would soon be photographing microfilm in someone's private jet or fighting off a horde of giant shrews. She wondered what conversations she would have with Drgnan, what they might talk about, whether he would tell her more about Delaware, so she could dream that she was there again. She looked forward to everything that would happen, so long as the four of them could be together.

So she was happy when, late at night, they pulled off the highway and spun down an off-ramp; when they passed the Halt 'n' Buy she knew was hers, and the O'Dermott's Drive-thru, and the Fashion Hole. She was happy when they drove past the center of Pelt, with its post office like any post office and its town hall like any town hall. She was happy when they passed a soccer field and went down a dip and past a fake stone wall. And she was happy when they pulled into the driveway of a house that looked like every other house in the neighborhood—because, though it looked like any other house, the people who ran out of it, crying with relief, were the people she loved—and this house, in this place, at this time, was home.

APPENDIX

ADDITIONAL LYRICS TO
"THE SONG THAT NEVER ENDS"

This is the song that never ends,

It just goes on and on, my friends.

Some people started singing it, not knowing what it was,

And they'll continue singing it forever just because

This is the song that never ends,

It just goes on and on, my friends.

Some people started singing it, not knowing what it was,

And they'll continue singing it forever just because

This is the song that never ends,

It just goes on and on, my friends.

Some people started singing it, not knowing what it was,

And they'll continue singing it forever just because

This is the song that never ends,

It just goes on and on, my friends.

Some people started singing it, not knowing what it was,

And they'll continue singing it forever just because

This is the song that never ends,

It just goes on and on, my friends.

Some people started singing it, not knowing what it was,

And they'll continue singing it forever just because

This is the song that never ends,

It just goes on and on, my friends.

Some people started singing it, not knowing what it was,

And they'll continue singing it forever just because

This is the song that never ends,

It just goes on and on, my friends.

Some people started singing it, not knowing what it was,

And they'll continue singing it forever just because

This is the song that never ends,

It just goes on and on, my friends.

Some people started singing it, not knowing what it was,

And they'll continue singing it forever just because

This is the song that never ends,

It just goes on and on, my friends.

Some people started singing it, not knowing what it was,

And they'll continue singing it forever just because

This is the song that never ends,

It just goes on and on, my friends.

Some people started singing it, not knowing what it was,

And they'll continue singing it forever just because

This is the song that never ends,

It just goes on and on, my friends.

Some people started singing it, not knowing what it was,

And they'll continue singing it forever just because

This is the song that never ends,

It just goes on and on, my friends.

Some people started singing it, not knowing what it was,

And they'll continue singing it forever just because

This is the song that never ends,

It just goes on and on, my friends.

Some people started singing it, not knowing what it was,

And they'll continue singing it forever just because

This is the song that never ends,

It just goes on and on, my friends.

Some people started singing it, not knowing what it was,

And they'll continue singing it forever just because

This is the song that never ends,

It just goes on and on, my friends.

Some people started singing it, not knowing what it was,

And they'll continue singing it forever just because

This is the song that never ends,

It just goes on and on, my friends.

Some people started singing it, not knowing what it was,

And they'll continue singing it forever just because